CW00766928

Dear Cheryl,

IT IS SOMETHING
TO HAVE BEEN

Carly Schabowski

Best wishes

Holland House

Carly Schabowski

Copyright © 2016 by Carly Schabowski

Carly Schabowski asserts her moral right to be identified as
the author of this book. All rights reserved. This book or
any portion thereof may not be reproduced or used in any
manner whatsoever without the express written permission of
the publisher except for the use of brief quotations in a book
review.

All characters appearing in this work are fictitious. Any
resemblance to real persons, living or dead, is purely
coincidental. Any characters denoted by government office are
entirely fictional and not based on any official, appointed
or elected.

Paperback ISBN: 9781910688137
Kindle: 9781910688144

Illustrations: B. Lloyd
Cover picture: Alice Pennefather
Cover design by Ken Dawson, Creative Covers
Typeset by handebooks.co.uk

Published in the UK

Holland House Books
Holland House
47 Greenham Road
Newbury, Berkshire RG14 7HY
United Kingdom

www.hhousebooks.com

Supported using public funding by
ARTS COUNCIL
ENGLAND

LOTTERY FUNDED

For Stan and Roma

It is something to have wept as we have wept,
It is something to have done as we have done,
It is something to have watched when all men slept,
And seen the stars which never see the sun.

It

is

something

to

have

wept

The Departure – September 1942

The morning of my departure the weather had turned: summer was over. Rain fell in heavy drops that soon clogged up the gutters and filled potholes, transforming them into small lakes. I stood outside the café underneath a wooden awning, watching the grey waves roll one on top of the other, the boats straining against the taut ropes of their moorings and pitching fiercely into the orange buoys that bobbed between them.

The awning leaked. Dashes of water sporadically fell onto my cigarette so that it crackled as I smoked. I checked the time – it was three o'clock, I didn't have long to wait now. A part of me knew that you were not going to come, but I waited nonetheless – hoping we could end this differently, hoping I could say goodbye.

Eva came to see me off in the end. We sat in the café, the windows steamed up from the heat of the damp bodies, pressed closely together around tea-stained tables so that it felt as if there was no air left in the whole room. Eva ordered tea and did not drink it. I drank my tea, black with one sugar, and watched as she played with the new gold band on her finger; it looked dull under the cheap, harsh lighting.

'Do you want a cigarette?' she asked me, shaking one from the packet for herself.

'Yes. Outside, though. I can't breathe in here.'

She nodded and followed me. I expected her to complain about the rain, but she said nothing. I lit her cigarette for her and she watched the boats bucking.

'Glynn's gone,' I said.

'Yes. Two days ago.'

'You'll be alright,' I said. I wanted to reassure my sister, the girl who would read my stories as a child and laugh when she noticed that her name appeared in every one.

'Yes,' she replied. 'I'll be fine.' She blew a cloud of smoke in front of her.

'You'll see Ma?'

'Tomorrow. Harry,' she suddenly turned to me, 'you'll be alright too?'

'Yes. I'll be fine. So will Glynn. You'll see.'

Eva waited on the dock and watched the hulk of the ship navigate its way out of the mouth of the harbour. I watched her watch me until she was a speck on the shoreline. I squinted to see her until the shoreline became a dot too, and all I was left with were the gloomy waves rolling one on top of the other.

*****

Berneray
January 20 1946

It was the morning of my twenty-third birthday, and I woke lying on the cold wooden floor of the cottage, dressed in someone else's clothes. For a moment, I felt the rush of cold water over my body, pulling me down, then I realised it was the breeze beneath the door. I lay there for what seemed like hours, staring at the thin spider cracks in the white-washed ceiling, trying to collect my thoughts.

I had been on the island of Berneray now for two days and was still wearing the clothes I had been given by my father – his cast-offs. The day I arrived the rain had fallen so heavily that I could barely see the path leading from the jetty up the small grassy slope to the house. Once inside, I had been so grateful for the simple dryness, that I made my bed on the floor near the fireplace with every intention of building a fire. But whether it was the journey over the rough sea or the exhaustion of the past few years, I fell asleep there and barely moved since.

Perhaps you are wondering why I chose to come here—and last night, as the wind slammed against the shutters and rattled the chimney pot on the roof, I wondered this myself.

I had closed my eyes and listened to the roar of the wind, sweeping over the sheep-fleeced fields and hitting the small house that stood in its way, and realised that there was nowhere else for me to go.

January 23 1946

You see, when I look back on those days, I realise that I had very little choice of where to go. My parents could not contain me and my nightmares in their house – those dreams where the water engulfed me, filling my lungs, whilst I saw the faces of the dead float past.

London was so grey and ruined that I felt if I stayed, I would certainly go mad. I realised too that I knew no-one anymore. Those men who had become like family over the past few years were either dead or home with their true loved ones, and those who had stayed behind whilst I had rocked about on those endless seas did not know me anymore; I was a stranger to everyone, including myself.

This morning, I picked up a pen to write to you, my

dearest Mary, then put it back down knowing that it was pointless; it was a letter you could never receive. Instead, I picked up my diary. This I can write; this I can do.

Writing used to come so easily to me. I would barely notice the flick of my pen across the paper, forming stories, songs, poems, love notes, all of which you would read back to me, telling me how you loved them, telling me how you loved me. Now, the writing is harder. Each movement is deliberate, each letter is painful, each sentence I dread to read back. But I do it, I write, because my dearest Mary, what else do I have? Everything else has washed away.

March 1946

I am alone. I am lonely. I'm not the first person to say those words, nor write them. But, I wonder, can I take credit for them as being entirely mine? On this island, which is made up of sheep and a scattering of farmers and their wives, who live miles from me and don't speak to me even when I see them, can I claim those words? Alone. Lonely.

Surely the word *lonely* I can claim. Eva is now alone too so that word cannot be mine, but *lonely*, that can be mine. Eva cannot know this loneliness: this loneliness where I sit and watch the sheep eat the grass side-by-side, and feel envious that they have something – someone next to them.

I try not to sleep on the floor as often now; instead, I have made peace with the single bed and fall into it when I have exhausted myself writing and walking. The wallpaper in the bedroom is too busy—the small crimson and purple flowers dance madly when I stare at them until I feel I am on a boat again, pitching left and right, so I have to lie down in front of the fireplace, feeling the reassuring wood underneath me – the solid ground.

August 1946

Philip stood looking down at me. 'You're sleeping on the floor,' he said, then stepped over me and walked into the kitchen.

'Coffee? Tea?' he shouted.

'Yes,' I answered. I rubbed my eyes and sat up.

'Here,' Philip came back into the room and gave me a glass of water.

'I thought you were making tea?'

'It's too hot for tea. It's summer out there if you haven't realised already.'

'Oh,' I said. No, I hadn't noticed. It made no difference at night when the water in my dreams was still freezing.

He ruffled some papers on my desk then sat in the armchair and pulled at his green tie, making it come away from underneath the fat of his chin.

'That's better,' he said. 'So bloody hot. Why on earth have you got the fire lit?'

'I like it.'

He shook his head and took a large gulp of water.

'I got your package,' he said eventually.

'Oh.'

'It's good. All of it. I'd like to see the rest.'

'I've not finished it.'

'Well, you can finish it in a nice flat in Mayfair Harry, and stop all this nonsense living with sheep as your neighbours.'

'I like it here.'

'Harry,' he said, gently now, 'you're a writer. It's time.'

Summer

Eva cycled past the field of sunflowers that bobbed their heads in the afternoon breeze. The heatwave had dried the usual mud into a fine yellow sand that her tyres now stirred up, filling the air around her.

At first, all she saw was a small brown shape, hazy through the powdery air. She stopped pedalling and walked a few yards back down the track. She saw that the shape was a worn brown leather boot sitting on its own. She picked up the boot, looked at it and set it back down. She glanced over her shoulder back toward the town and then ahead of her. Then she picked up the boot again, placed it in the wicker basket on the front of her bicycle and covered it with her light blue cardigan.

She pedalled quickly, covering the mile home faster than she had in months. She cycled past the vicar who stood outside the church speaking to a parishioner she didn't know. She turned a corner quickly and almost ran over Max, Cynthia's dog. Cynthia shouted from her garden, half hidden amongst the thick bushes of roses. Eva rang the bell on her bike by way of apology and cycled on.

A few minutes later, she arrived home to her cottage, rested the bike against the fence, took the boot from the basket, and walked inside.

The house was stuffy from the day's heat. She opened the living room windows and walked into the kitchen. Setting the boot down on the kitchen table, Eva poured herself a glass of water and stood next to the sink, eyeing the boot suspiciously.

It reminded her of a soldier's boot but it seemed slightly longer, with a thick sole and heel. There was mud on the heel, and the fine dust from the sunflower field had covered it, making it a lighter brown than its original colour. She shook her head and felt slightly foolish for taking it. It seemed bigger and less significant here.

She picked it up to throw away, then stopped herself as she reached the bin. She looked at it again, and shaking her head, opened a cupboard above the bread bin and put the boot inside. Then, she washed her hands in the kitchen sink and made herself a potted meat sandwich. She walked into her small living room, sat in the floral armchair by the stale, empty fireplace, and ate slowly. When she had finished she leaned back in her chair and closed her eyes, listening to the late afternoon cries of birds and the hum of crickets in the dried grass.

The brass clock on the mantelpiece chimed six just as Viv arrived. She didn't knock, but let herself in and stood in front of Eva, breathing heavily.

'You'll never guess,' she said, sitting down in the green armchair by the bay window and rolling up her cream dress, exposing her large calves and dry-skinned knees.

'What?'

'They've found a body!'

'Where?'

'In the sunflower field,' Viv replied. 'No-one we know, anyway.'

'Who is it then?'

'Oh, no idea. A man. George in the corner shop says he thinks he was a tramp. Usual story, George says; deserter in the war, nowhere to go. It's to be expected I suppose.' She picked up a newspaper from the low coffee table and fanned herself. 'This heat!'

'Do you want a drink?' Eva asked. 'Water?'

'Surely it's time for something stronger?'

Eva walked into the kitchen and poured a finger of gin into a heavy crystal glass. She topped the drink off with tonic and a slice of lemon, wishing she had ice.

'Bring food if you have any!' Viv shouted.

Eva took the tin of biscuits from the cupboard and put a few of the smaller broken ones into a flower-patterned bowl, a wedding gift from her marriage to Glynn six years ago; it was the only one out of a set of four which had survived.

She put the tin back into the cupboard, and her hand brushed against the boot. She closed the cupboard door and looked at her hand where a smear of fine yellow dust highlighted against the paleness of her skin. She felt her stomach do a slight leap and held onto the counter.

'You okay in there?' Viv shouted.

'Just a minute.' She wiped the back of her hand on her dress, pushed the boot further into the cupboard and stood back to see if she could see it, feeling an odd relief when she found she couldn't.

She walked into the living room, setting the drink and biscuits on the table next to Viv.

'It's so hot!' Viv said again. 'It's driving me crazy!'

Eva sat in her chair and watched Viv fiddling with the wedding ring that seemed embedded in her fleshy finger.

'Who found it?' Eva asked. 'Sorry, I mean him, not it.'

'No idea. Colin came home and told me.'

'How did he find out?'

'No idea.' Viv looked out of the window and swallowed her drink in one go.

'Another?' Eva asked.

'No. I'd better go.'

'Let me know if you hear anything else?'

Viv stood and grabbed a few biscuits out of the bowl. She walked to the front door. 'Will do,' she said, then almost as an afterthought, 'are you okay?'

'Yes,' Eva answered.

'Eat more. You're wasting away.' Viv opened the door and did not close it behind her.

Eva sat in the chair for ten minutes, then stood when the clock chimed half past. She closed the front door and walked into the kitchen. She opened the cupboard, and, standing on her tiptoes, reached in and pulled the boot out. She set it on the table and looked in a box by the kitchen door for a newspaper. Quickly, she wrapped the boot in the paper, walked into the garden and put it in the bottom of the bin.

She locked the door and saw the boot had left some of its yellow dust behind, so she filled the sink full of hot soapy water and spent the next half an hour scrubbing the table. When it was clean, she looked around the kitchen and scrubbed all the counters, then cleaned inside the cupboards, only stopping when she realised it was almost dark.

Eva switched on the hallway light and climbed the tightly curved staircase. At the top sat her small bedroom, still warm from the day's heat. She opened the window, and a sweet scented breeze filled the room. Lying on her bed, she kicked off her shoes but did not remove her clothes.

After a few minutes, her eyes closed, and she drifted

between sleep and waking, fitfully dreaming that her bedroom was covered in fine yellow dust and sunflowers grew from the walls. Every time she tried to cut the sunflowers away, more grew in their place. Feeling scared, she turned and tried to run away, but found her legs would not move as fast as she wanted them to. Then, she tripped. She looked at the floor, and her carpet had turned into a muddy bog with soldiers' boots half sunk into it. She bent down to pick the boots up, and as she held them, blood ran out from the inside staining the brown a deep rich red. She dropped the boots and saw a hand reach through the mire toward her, wanting her to rescue them. She knew the hand; the wedding band on his finger gave him away. She grabbed his hand and pulled, but felt herself sinking down—the mud and blood covering her up to her neck, slowly creeping over her mouth and nose.

She screamed and woke up. She sat on the edge of her bed and looked at her hands, expecting them to be stained red.

The church clock chimed eleven, and she ran down the stairs into the kitchen. Her hands shook as she inserted the key into the door, and she raced out into the night. The moon was full, lighting her garden enough for her to find the bin. She shoved her hands in amongst the rubbish and felt for the boot. Her hands felt potato peelings and something smooth and wet. Finally, her fingers curled around the newspaper bundle. She yanked it out and sat on the damp lawn, breathing heavily.

She walked inside, strode to the front door and pulled it open. She stood for a moment looking out, then turned into the living room. She picked up the bowl and tipped it upside down, letting the biscuits and crumbs scatter across the wooden floor. Wrapping the bowl together with the boot in the newspaper, she walked out into the night, forgetting to lock the door behind her.

She ran all the way to the track and only noticed she wasn't wearing shoes when she trod on a stone. Ignoring the pain in her foot, she ran on. She stopped once to catch her breath and sat on a grassy verge. Sweat trickled from the nape of her neck and began to cool, making her shiver. She looked about in the dark and could make out the old oak tree; she was not far now, another minute and she would be there. She stood and ran again – trying to ignore the stitch that had developed in her side and the pain of running in her bare feet– she sprinted toward the oak tree, finally turning right into the sunflower field crushing the flowers as she ran through. She fell to her hands and knees and scrabbled in the dirt, digging as fast as she could. Two nails broke as she worked, ripping off too low and taking skin with them. She felt her warm blood mix with the dry sand and felt sick.

An owl flew overhead and hooted as it followed its prey. She jumped and looked up at the sky.

'It's going to be alright,' she said.

When the dryness gave way to moist soil she stopped digging. She unwrapped the newspaper bundle, placed the boot in the hole and put the bowl on top. She covered them with soil and patted the mound gently, then stood and smoothed down the skirt of her dress, streaking it with dirt.

She walked home slowly, listening to the breeze blow through the stalks of the sunflowers. She imagined their heads nodding in approval as she passed them, and she smiled at the thought. When she reached her house she saw the front door was open and the downstairs lights were switched on.

She stepped cautiously inside, and in the living room saw Viv sitting in the green chair by the window, her dress rolled up, and this time exposing bruised knees. Her hair was messy and covered the left side of her face, where a red tint was just visible at the top of her cheekbone. Eva stood in front of her friend, and they eyed each other for a minute.

'You're sweating,' Viv said, eventually.

'It's still warm.'

'You need a glass of water.'

'Surely it's time for something stronger?' Eva asked.

Viv nodded.

Eva walked into the kitchen and washed her hands in the sink. She took two glasses, filled one with gin the other with tonic. She took the drink to her friend, sat in her armchair next to the stale, empty fireplace and placed her hand on her stomach, rubbing it gently.

'It's so hot,' Viv said, looking out of the window.

'Enough to make you crazy,' Eva said.

It

is

something

to

have

done

as

we

have

done

The flowers had grown since I last walked in the park, and I was too late for most. The season was creeping into autumn, the petals from the dahlias and pink and blue hydrangeas falling on the lawn, scattering themselves as if at a wedding.

I left the park at Hyde Corner, turning into Piccadilly. The waves of people never cease to unnerve me these days; they fill every space taking all the air so that I feel I am drowning. I struggled to find my place in amongst the human flow, stumbling every so often into the wrong lane, apologising as I bumped into people with busy lives.

Once I found my pace, I looked around: the rubble of the bombed buildings was being cleared and the city bit-by-bit placed back together. It seems to me sometimes that the whole of London is now a broken puzzle, the pieces lying all about; people too are scattered, and we are trying to fit and force the pieces together to create a new picture – perhaps something better.

Philip had suggested tea at The Ritz, and mentioned he had a surprise for me. No doubt with Philip this surprise consisted of an old bottle of scotch and the afternoon stretching into an evening of drinking.

My novel had sold well. Philip was wily, and as much as I admired his abilities there was a ruthlessness about him that made me wary. I wasn't quite sure how he had convinced people, who could barely scrape enough to eat from their ration books, to spend what little they had on my writing.

'It cheers them,' he had said. 'They need something to smile about.'

I reached the bulbed arches of The Ritz. The polished glass doors were held open for me by a liveried doorman, revealing the plush red carpet that looked as new as the day they laid it. The reception desk, made of heavy, shiny mahogany, stood between the lounge and me. A man dressed in a dark, discreetly expensive suit and black tie stood behind the desk, feigning busyness by shuffling papers; he silently nodded in my direction as I passed, not quite catching my eye.

Philip was sat near the window, his fleshy hands cupping a thick glass of amber whisky, and a woman and a small boy sat with him. As I approached I realised that the woman was Eva—her smile crooked and worry etched in her brow.

'Harry!' Philip's voice was loud. As he stood up and walked forward to greet me, his hand fussed with his tie, then smoothed his shirt into place. I sensed the other people in the room carefully not looking to see who caused such a stir.

I sat at the table.

'Hello Frank,' I said to my nephew. He looked at me with the intent gaze that he has inherited from his father, Glynn.

'Say hello to your uncle, Francis!' Philip scolded the boy.

'Hello,' he said sadly, and dropped his eyes to study the tablecloth.

'It's Francis now is it?' I asked.

'Sounds more appropriate – a touch of gravitas, don't you think?' Philip asked. It was impossible to tell if he was serious or joking – perhaps both.

I looked at Frank, who was now staring at the salt and pepper cruets, and wondered if anyone had asked if he wanted to change his name.

'I suppose you're wondering why we are here?' Eva

asked.

'Drinks first I think,' Philip's voice boomed.

As he looked around for a waiter, Eva placed her hand over Philip's. He turned to face her and I saw her smile.

'Harry,' she began, 'Philip and I are engaged.'

I glanced at her, then looked at my nephew, who would not look up; his fingers were busy tracing the delicate pattern on the cloth.

'Do you like to draw?' I asked him.

'Yes,' he muttered.

'What do you like to draw?'

'Plants, or flowers. Things outside—'

'Really Harry,' Philip interrupted. 'Is that all you can say? You talk to the child about drawing? We're getting married and thought you would be happy about it.'

'I am happy for you,' I said, looking at Eva. 'If you are both happy then so am I.'

'I am,' Eva said confidently. 'Francis needs a father, and Philip loves us both. We can be a proper family.'

'Well then. Congratulations to you both,' I said. My voice was not normal, I noticed. Somehow it had risen an octave or two, and was louder, as though I was trying to drown out the quiet murmuring and clinking sounds of the tea room. I tried again. 'We'll order champagne to celebrate!'

'That's the spirit!' Philip slapped me on the back.

The afternoon dragged by, and Philip naturally turned the conversation to my next novel. 'Cheery, Harry, that's what it needs to be.' He sucked on his cigar, the smoke making Francis' eyes water.

'I'm not sure what it will be just yet,' I said.

'It should be about new beginnings. New life.

Rebuilding. Look at us, all around, rebuilding London, our homes. That's what people want!'

'What about what made us have to rebuild in the first place?'

'I don't think you have to rake all that up Harry!' Philip shook his head. 'The historians do that and the newspapers pick over it endlessly. You do what you are good at. The last novel, the love story, worked well. Everyone likes a happy ending.'

'It was fictional,' I said.

'Yes, I know.' Philip looked at Eva. 'But, I suppose it doesn't have to be, does it? Things change.'

'What do you want to write, Uncle Harry?' Frank was staring at me.

'I want to write about people,' I said.

'People like us?'

'Yes. People like us. Especially people like us. I think we are interesting, aren't we?'

He considered this question. 'I don't think I'm interesting, but I think things I look at are interesting. Plants are interesting. They grow, but then they die. That's interesting don't you think?'

'I do,' I said. My nephew understood me at six-years-old. Maybe I should write the book just for him.

'Silly talk for a boy your age!' Philip was booming again. 'You should read this lovely little book about trains that I have. A good book for boys.'

Frank looked at the tablecloth again.

'Won't that be nice?' Eva asked him, gently placing the tip of her finger under his chin, raising his head to meet her gaze. They both seemed conscious of a kind of betrayal in her words. I watched them look at each other for a moment;

Frank held her gaze. He nodded ever so slightly at her, as if she had said something else – something secret between the two of them, something to make him happy to agree.

'Yes.' Frank answered. 'Thank you, Mr Ainsworth.'

'None of this Mister nonsense anymore, my boy. You can call me Father.'

There was a silence. Then Philip laughed, and Eva smiled worriedly.

I left at six, leaving the trio to have dinner alone. I wished I could take Frank, or Francis with me: I felt for the boy. I wondered how he would adapt to his new father, his new life, and whether Philip could be the father he needed. Would Philip try to buy his love, I wondered, with puppies, toys and sweets? Or would he advise the boy, be his friend, wipe away his tears? My hand twitched and I wished for a pen so I could write Frank's story for him, and show him how it could be with a new father, how he could be happy again—if only the stories could come true.

I walked back through the park on my way home, taking a last look at the flowers before autumn arrived and blanketed the ground with its decaying leaves.

Growing pains

Frank played outside every day, taking with him a little black-and-white terrier they had given him to ease the transition of the new home and new father. He took the train, which his new father had given him too, and sat at the bottom of the garden behind the fruit bushes so that no-one could see him. Not that anyone would come to look for him, but this was private – secret, his own.

It had started a year ago, when he had seen his mother crying in front of a vase of white lilies. He hadn't understood why the lilies made her sad, and when he asked her, she told him that they reminded her of a sad day. Lilies, she told him, were not happy flowers.

He had wondered then, what were happy flowers? At the library, he borrowed a book about gardening and studied the pictures: roses looked happy to him, but they seemed hard to grow; he read Latin names of *Biguonia Radicans,* a trumpet vine, and decided that this would be good, but then he realised that it lived mostly in America. He thought that maybe one day he would go to America to see this creeping trumpet flower. He turned another page and found *Campanula,* a bellflower. He liked the shape and the curve of the petals and thought that no-one could look at this and feel sad. This would be the first he would plant. Next he chose sweet peas and marigolds, mostly as they were easy to grow and he could leave them to fend for themselves. The last flower he chose was a sunflower. Everyone liked sunflowers, he knew, and to see its tall happy face peeking out from over the bushes every morning would surely make his mother smile.

It was now late August and his little patch behind the hedge had bloomed: pinks, purples and golden yellow all mixed together to cover the patch of soil he had selected. The sunflower had grown, but was not tall enough to display its bright message over the hedge. He had tried to get his mother to come and see them all at the beginning of the month, but she was busy getting ready to go away on a honeymoon with her new husband – his new father.

'I'll look at your surprise when I get back,' she promised, and kissed him lightly on the cheek before her proud husband whisked her away to Paris.

Now they had come home, but Frank had changed his mind about showing her his secret. He enjoyed the solitude of this oasis, enjoyed the pruning, the neatening of the soil and the watering, using a can he had found in the shed. He could sit for hours with his little dog Bailey at his side, chatting to him about what he was growing, imagining both himself and the dog as gardeners one day. 'You can dig the holes,' Frank told the dog, who cocked his head to the side as his master spoke. 'Then I'll plant and at the end of the day we'll sit and eat biscuits and drink lemonade.' The dog licked his lips in agreement.

In mid-September the weather turned unseasonably cold, and Frank saw his flowers begin to die. Only the sunflower still held on, but soon it too began to droop. One afternoon, he sat in the living room looking out into the cold garden and began to cry.

'What's wrong?' his mother asked him, wrapping herself around him.

'They're dying, all of them,' he sobbed.

'What are?'

Frank looked at his mother and took her by the hand to his secret garden.

'It was meant to be a surprise,' he said. 'Now look, they're all dying.'

His mother did not speak. He looked at her and saw that she was staring at the sunflower. She reached out her hand and stroked its drooping petals as if trying to soothe them. He noticed that she was crying too; silent tears that she didn't seem to notice.

'Don't you like it?' he asked. 'I thought sunflowers were happy?'

She turned to look at him and smiled. 'They are,' she said.

Without another word, she took him inside and made him warm milk. His new father followed her into the kitchen, and Frank watched as he hugged her and wiped her face. Then he turned to look at Frank and walked toward him.

'I didn't do anything!' Frank said, panicked.

'Calm down boy!' his new father boomed. 'I know you didn't. Your mother said that you are sad that your plants are dying?'

'Yes sir,' Frank answered.

'Well, don't be. They are just sleeping now, that's what happens in autumn, then next spring they will bloom back into life again, you'll see.' He patted Frank on the shoulder and walked away.

Frank sat with his warm milk and his dog at his side, and decided that this new father wasn't as bad as he had originally thought – so long as he was telling the truth, of course.

'Are you alright?' his mother asked him.

'Yes,' he said. 'I was just thinking that maybe I will call him Father now, is that alright?'

His mother smiled and kissed the top of his head.

'See Bailey,' he whispered to his dog, 'all we needed were some happy flowers.'

It

is

something

to

have

hungered

It was snowing. Thick swathes fell, blanketing the street within hours. I sat in my chair in the study, watching it, wondering if it would put everyone off.

The caterers had made it, however. Slogging through the frozen mounds and turning the whiteness into grey slush, they arrived laden with the cut crystal glasses, boxes of champagne and silver trays of canapés; for a moment I was taken back to my wedding day: Barbara smiling by my side, our small son at her heels.

I opened the first bottle of champagne, as though celebrating or avoiding the memory. The clock on the mantelpiece chimed three as I drank, the bubbles tickling my throat. I felt almost immediate relief; my shoulders slackened and my hands felt looser; I poured another.

By the time the doorbell rang at seven and Philip strode in, I was on to the second bottle, and a smile (hopefully charming, but possibly manic) was on my face.

'Ah, Philip you made it!' I said. I was happy to see him. Over the years, I had warmed to him and his ways. He had proven himself to be a good husband and father, whereas I had made a disaster of my personal life. Yet, he hadn't judged me, and stood by me through it all. I walked over to him and took him in an embrace—usually an awkward thing for me to accomplish.

He slapped me on the back and pulled quickly away.

'Drink?' I asked.

'When did you start?'

'Ah, time. No idea. It's a lovely day,' I pointed at the whitewashed street. I poured him a glass of champagne.

'Eva's not coming,' he said.

'No matter. No matter. How's Francis doing? He was such a good boy.'

'He's got a job, quite settled now over in America.' Philip sat down. 'Not a boy now.'

'Yes quite. No. Quite. Not a boy. A man. Yes – I remember now. Went to Virginia didn't he? Off to the land of the free and the freedom to dream and all that. Freedom. Lovely girls, American girls. Funny,' I jabbered. I sat across from him and smiled. He drummed his fingers on the armrest and looked around the study, eyeing my desk— void of the typewriter and the usual stacks of papers.

'Another party then,' he said eventually.

'Yes, well, you know,' I wiped my brow, 'single man and all that again. The quintessential bachelor, The Times called me.'

'Yes, I read it.'

'What did you think?'

'I think you need to write.'

'I will, I will.' I waved my hand in the air dismissively. 'All in good time, Philip, you know me. I always produce the work in the end.'

'It's been two years. And so far, you have managed to pop up in the gossip pages more than the book pages.' Philip placed his glass on the side table and leaned forward, clasping his hands together. 'I worry,' he said.

'About what?'

'You. Not writing. It's not healthy.'

'Come on Philip, it's meant to be a party. Relax, would you? They'll all be here soon. Our friends. It'll be a blast, you'll see.'

'Your first novel sold very well Harry. The second and the third were equally as good. It's time for a fourth, don't you think? Even those short stories you are always scribbling away at could be printed rather than a quote from you about a new restaurant opening!'

'Philip, you need to stop worrying, honestly. I'll write a new novel soon. No need to publish the short stories; they're more of a diary anyway,' I said. 'Goodness, when have I ever let you down before? The first novel was written in a matter of months I'll remind you! Just after you picked me up from sleeping on that cold floor on Berneray!'

Philip laughed at the memory. 'You've come a long way since then Harry, I'll admit it.'

'Why thank you!'

'I just don't want you to go back to where you started, that's all. What with Barbara leaving and taking the boy, you know you didn't do too well the last time.'

'That was worse,' I answered, thinking of Mary.

'Indeed, of course, I'm sorry to bring her up again. Of course it was worse. But all I mean is that you are not doing too well now.'

I rubbed my forehead. Why did he have to bring it all up again? Those years were behind me – those years of the endless arguments about work, about not spending time with the boy, about the drinking. It was all behind me: the war, Mary, the pretending to be a family with Barbara— pretending I loved her as I loved Mary. On cue, my left leg began to hurt; the shrapnel moving its way toward the skin reminding me that I could still feel pain no matter what. I rubbed it.

'See,' Philip said, nodding at my leg.

'It's the cold,' I said, nodding toward the snow-coated window panes. 'Please Philip, just trust me. I'm working on something at the moment. Similar to the first novel – something about loss and redemption, but with comedy. That's what you want, isn't it? Just wait and see. It'll be good, I promise.'

Philip loosened his tie, picked up his glass, and smiled. 'I'm sure it will be.'

By the time the doorbell rang to signal the first of the guests, Philip and I were back on good terms and had managed to finish the second bottle. I wondered whether he believed my lie or not, but I thought if I poured enough champagne down him, he would soon forget what I had said.

'Millie!' I cried, as Millicent Smith entered, draped head to toe in a white Grecian dress, a silver brooch on the shoulder. She looked splendid. She hugged us both, filling our noses with her strong flowery scent.

'I thought I'd match the weather,' she said, twirling in her dress; it was like a beautiful snowstorm in the house. 'You know darling, I can't quite stand the new fashion. Gerald and I went to a party last night, flared trousers everywhere, flowery shirts and headbands, and that was just the men!' she cried.

I handed her a glass of champagne. 'No danger of flowery shirts here,' I said, stroking down my white dress shirt.

'No, I can always count on you both to uphold decent wear for men. You know there were drugs too?'

'What kind?'

'Does it matter?' Philip looked at me.

'Not really,' I muttered and swallowed another mouthful of bubbles.

'Where's Gerald?' Philip asked.

'Oh, he'll be here in a minute. He's gone to walk the Gregsons from the corner. Not sure why he thinks that Margaret can't make it on her own.' She frowned. 'I mean she's got her husband to help her. Although, if you speak to Suzie tonight, she may tell you what she told me, which is that it turns out that poor Margaret's husband is playing away, if you know what I mean.' She winked at Philip and drained her glass. 'Still, I don't know why Gerald has to help her. The snow isn't that thick.' She looked at the front door.

'You know who I saw the other day,' Philip steered her away from Margaret, 'Felicity. Apparently she's got cancer.'

Millie whipped her head round, almost breaking her slender neck. 'Cancer?'

'Apparently.' Philip stood up and walked to the kitchen to get another bottle.

The champagne had taken its effect by now, and I tried to focus on Millie as she told me what she knew about cancer, and how she heard that hippies were smoking marijuana, and that Margaret was obviously looking to play away herself, and did I know that Jilly and Martin had gone to Australia?

I shook my head, and as I did, Mille became a blur of white. I felt sick.

'Here.' Philip was back and handed me a glass of water. 'I told the waiters to bring some canapés round. You need to eat.'

I nodded at him and drank the water in one.

I wasn't sure when the party really started; it is possible that I fell asleep at some point. But suddenly the house was full of people, some of whom I knew and the vast majority of whom I didn't. My mouth was dry but thankfully my head felt a little clearer.

I stood up and joined the throng, picking up a glass of champagne from a passing waiter. I was paying for this after all.

'So, what's the next great novel going to be then?' a voice boomed at me. It was Margaret's husband, a banker if memory served me right. His face was round and red, and I imagined that he had been born that way, fat, bald, red: what a disappointment for his parents.

'I'm not sure yet.'

'Ah now come on! You're amongst friends here. Come on tell us, give us a hint. What did The Times call you? The voice of the new generation? Come on writer!' he demanded. 'What are you writing?'

'I'm going to write about people having affairs,' I deadpanned and walked away.

Philip was standing in the corner talking to Felicity, a thinner, paler Felicity than I remembered. She smiled at me, the sparkle still in her eyes. I'd leave them to it, I decided.

I went from group to group, taking in snippets of information and not quite understanding who or what they were talking about. I drank more, nodded when they nodded, smiled when they smiled and laughed when they laughed, but felt as if I wasn't really in the room at all. Trying to follow a rather long-winded joke, I felt a light touch on my arm. Felicity. I turned and followed her out of the room.

'I just wanted to say thank you for tonight,' she said, taking her coat from the stand.

'You're leaving already?' Suddenly, and quite inexplicably, I felt sad. I didn't want her to leave.

'It's after midnight.' She looked at the grandfather clock.

So it was. I shook my head.

'Harry,' she placed her pale, almost see-through hand

on my arm, 'are you all right?'

'No,' I said. I felt a burning in my eyes.

'You know, all these people, most of them are not your friends. They won't help you.'

'I'm lonely,' I said.

'I know. Maybe writing will help? You need to work. You need to have something.'

'I don't know what to write,' I said.

Surprisingly she laughed. 'Oh Harry, don't be so silly! You've always written about life, about people—and look around you, life's everywhere. There are stories everywhere. You just have to look. Why, even write about yourself Harry if you can't think of anything else. Write about what you did wrong and what you did right in life. See where you can make it better?'

She kissed me lightly on the cheek and walked through the front door into the snowy night. I knew somehow that I would never see her again.

I stood at the front door watching the snow fall for a while. A waiter offered me a fresh glass of champagne; I took it and stepped outside, my feet crunching the ice and snow as I walked into the communal gardens and stood in the middle listening to the quiet. I had never heard silence like this in London before.

My wife had taken my son.

I said it aloud, 'My wife has taken my son.' My voice echoed around the garden and didn't sound like my own. I took a sip of the champagne. The alcohol made me feel sick and tired—she was never going to come back: not Barbara, not Mary, not Glynn, not my son. They were all gone and I wished that I had been as lucky as Glynn and never come back either. Was it all my fault?

I took another sip. This time, the relaxing sensation it usually provided was gone. I looked at my glass, at the champagne bubbling as the flakes fell into it. Slowly I tipped the glass upside down, letting it pour onto the ground. I held the empty glass and walked in circles around the lawn. I trod carefully, trying to step back into the deep footsteps I had already made. A church clock somewhere in the city chimed two, and I made my way back to the party.

As I entered it seemed to me as though no-one had moved: they stood in their own circles, laughing and drinking, and only the waiters seemed to be different. They moved more slowly than before, two hands holding trays now instead of one, their eyes red from cigarette smoke and tiredness.

Philip came over and slapped me hard on the back. 'Having a good time?' he slurred.

'It's time for everyone to leave,' I said. I walked away from the scene, my wet shoes squelching on the wooden floor and leaving puddles as I walked up the stairs.

'Harry, what's wrong with your shoes?' Philip shouted.

I reached the spare bedroom and switched on the light. The large wooden wardrobe stood at the end of the bed. I opened it and took out my typewriter. Sitting on the bed, I fed a fresh piece of paper into it and began to write. Doing as Felicity had told me to, I began with my own story, writing about what I did wrong and hoping she was right, that it would make it all better...

The meeting had run late, and it was nearly eight o'clock when Harvey pulled into the gravelled driveway, not noticing that his wife's car was missing.

Dads

The meeting had run late, and it was nearly eight o'clock when Harvey pulled into the gravelled driveway, not noticing that his wife's car was missing. He took his son's birthday present from the passenger seat and walked to the black-lacquered front door. As soon as he opened the door, he knew something was wrong. The long, wide hallway was dark, and there was no pitter-patter of his children's small feet echoing over the wooden floor. He stood still for a moment, then dropped his briefcase by the coat stand and walked into the living room.

There was a note on the low coffee table, and he picked it up. He ran his hand over his name spelled out in his wife's familiar looped letters and put it back.

He sat in his favourite leather armchair, but did not extend the footrest nor lean back comfortably. Instead, he perched on the edge, holding the present, in its blue wrapping paper, tightly to his chest. He sat staring at the letter until it was dark outside, and all he could see in the living room were hazy grey shapes.

Harvey stood up and switched on the lamp. He pulled shut the heavy gold curtains and turned on the television. There was a soap on, something that Claire would normally watch. He turned the volume up, then walked into the kitchen and flicked the main light switch.

The fridge was covered in his children's finger paintings, and he looked at them for a minute, then opened the door. He stared at the heavily laden shelves, picked up some cheese, then put it back and closed the door.

He walked into the dining room and switched on the light, then mounted the stairs two-at-a-time and looked in each bedroom, turning on lights as he went. Finally, he walked slowly back down the stairs and again sat in his chair. After a few minutes, Harvey picked up the letter and read it. He screwed it into a ball and threw it at the bin in the corner of the room. He missed, and it rolled under the bookshelf, but he took no notice. He stood up and carried his son's present into the kitchen. He put the present on the table, took a glass from the cupboard and a bottle of scotch from the drinks cabinet. Harvey walked back into the living room, sat in front of the loud television and drank the scotch until he fell asleep.

The next morning, he woke, still in the armchair, with a spill of scotch on his white shirt. He opened and closed his eyes a few times—testing them. Then he slowly moved his arms and legs, feeling pain with every movement. With a little effort, he finally stood, then slowly made his way over to the side table and switched off the lamp. He walked into the kitchen and dining room and switched off the lights; now and again, he stopped to lean on furniture to steady himself.

Harvey stood at the bottom of the stairs for a few minutes and stretched his neck from side-to-side. Slowly, he made his way up the stairs, holding tightly onto the bannister.

He took off his clothes in his bathroom and stepped into the shower. The water was cold, but he didn't care and made himself hold his head under the icy stream until it was almost numb. He washed quickly and stepped out, letting himself drip-dry onto the bath mat, then he looked in the mirror and stared at his face until he didn't recognise it anymore.

The clothes he chose for work were not his usual choices of crisp shirt and tie. Instead, he opted for an old pair of cream trousers and a polo shirt.

Downstairs, he didn't bother with coffee or breakfast; he went straight out to his car and sat behind the wheel.

Blinking a few times in the bright sunlight, he looked for his sunglasses in the glove compartment, but couldn't find them. Instead, he found his son's soft toy—a monkey—wedged behind a road map. He held it for a moment then put the monkey in his lap and reversed quickly out of the driveway.

It wasn't far to the corner shop. He parked outside the front door and walked quickly inside. He chose two bottles of vodka and a bottle of the most expensive scotch. He paid and the man behind the counter raised his eyebrows at him.

'Birthday party,' Harvey said.

He nodded. Harvey used two plastic bags to carry the bottles to the car.

Climbing into his Mercedes he saw his son's monkey had fallen into the footwell, so he picked it up, put it in the passenger seat and pulled the seatbelt across it. He looked at the monkey and smiled.

He drove home, but couldn't remember doing it. He got out of the car and opened the passenger door. Undoing the seatbelt, he gently lifted the monkey out, then grabbed the two bags from of the boot and went inside the house.

He sat the monkey in his daughter's high chair in the

kitchen and put his son's present in front of it on the plastic tray. He rummaged around in the drawers and cupboards until he found a party hat from his 40th birthday. He sat the hat on top of the monkey's head, but it fell off. He stood for a minute, looking at the soft toy, then tried again, this time tying the string tight under the toy's head. He found some paper cups and poured vodka into one and juice into the other. He passed the cup of juice to the monkey.

'No vodka for you!' he said. He laughed and felt a little better.

He drank some more vodka and went into the living room. He turned on the television and switched the channel. Top of The Pops had just started and a young girl was dancing around on stage in luminous clothes, singing about her broken heart. He didn't like it, but went into the kitchen and looked at the monkey and nodded. Harvey then went back into the living room and turned the volume higher.

For the next few hours, Harvey drank straight vodka in the kitchen with his son's monkey, then drank scotch in the living room, sitting on the edge of his chair and staring at the television. He slept in the afternoon for a while, then woke up and decided he didn't want to be awake.

Harvey made his way upstairs, looked in the bathroom cabinet and found some sleeping tablets. He took a few, washed them down with scotch, and lay on the cool tiles of the bathroom.

In the evening, his doorbell rang. He opened his eyes but couldn't see properly, and his head felt full of cotton wool. The doorbell rang again, and he shouted for his wife. He sat up slowly and propped himself against the bathtub. Harvey felt confused. He looked at his hands and tried to count his fingers but got to four and couldn't remember what came next.

The bell rang again, and again he shouted for Claire.

He continued to try and count his fingers; he knew they would get him to ten, and he knew that once he got there it meant that he was okay. This time he got to six, then he realised that the doorbell had stopped ringing. Claire must have answered the door, he thought. He shouted for her to help him and, after a few minutes, he shakily got to his feet and decided to look for her and the children.

Using the walls to bounce off, he made his way into each neatly made-up bedroom and stared at the empty beds, wondering where they all were. He tried to walk downstairs, but couldn't, so he sat on the top step and pushed himself down on his backside, like he had told his son to stop doing. At the bottom of the stairs, he sat and shouted for Claire to help him. He put his head in his hands and waited for a few minutes. He tried to think of where they were and couldn't remember them leaving.

He thought of a film he had seen when a family was kidnapped and wondered if Claire had kidnapped the children, or if someone had taken them all including her. He tried to concentrate for a minute, tried to remember if his family had been kidnapped, or if it was just the movie that he was thinking of.

'My wife has taken my children,' he said out loud, reality settling on him. He knew deep down that he had made them leave, he had done this; he was solely to blame. After a minute or two, he decided that he needed to be punished for what he had done and he crawled to the phone that sat on the table near the front door. He dialled 999.

Harvey awoke to a police officer standing over him; all around voices were coming from radios and bright lights were blinding him.

'What's happening?' he asked. His mouth felt dry.

'Sir, can you tell me what's happened?'

He shook his head and felt a little sick.

The policeman looked away from him and murmured something to a female colleague.

'What did you say?' Harvey asked.

'Nothing sir,' he said. 'What's your name?'

'Harvey.'

'And what happened, Harvey?' The policeman sat on the stair next to him.

'My children are gone.'

'Did someone take them?'

Harvey nodded. 'My wife, I think.'

The officer waved over his colleague and whispered something into her ear.

'What did you say?' Harvey asked.

'I'm just telling her that it's all okay. That your family is safe.'

Harvey nodded.

'Have you been drinking, Harvey?'

'It was a birthday,' he said.

'Okay. Well, I think you need to sober up a little. Do you have anyone we could call for you?'

'No. I don't think so.'

'Okay then Harvey. What we will do, is let you sleep it off and come and check on you in a few hours, okay?'

He nodded.

'You do understand though, Harvey, that you can't ring the police like that again?'

The officer stood up, and Harvey saw him smile at his colleague.

'Goodnight, sir,' the officers said, almost in unison.

Harvey stood up shakily and made his way to the door. He saw that the lock was hanging off from where they had barged their way in. He walked into the dining room, dragged a heavy chair from the table and wedged it against the door handle.

He staggered into the kitchen and saw the monkey in the high chair, its party hat hanging limply off its head. He walked to the sink and threw up.

Harvey vomited until there was nothing left in his stomach but bile, and then slept on the couch for twelve hours.

When he woke, it was mid-afternoon. He sat for a while and wondered if it had been a dream. He looked around and saw the empty bottle of scotch lying on its side, the amber liquid creating a pool on the hardwood floor. He groaned loudly, then realised that the police officers had never checked on him.

'Bastards,' he said.

He cleaned the house as best he could; his head banged with every movement, and his stomach would not settle. When he had finished cleaning, he showered, dressed, ate some stale bread and cheese and lay on the couch, staring at the ceiling. Then he remembered that the door needed to be fixed. He found the yellow pages and a phone number for a locksmith who said they would be around in the next hour.

While he waited, he called work. 'I've got flu,' he said to his secretary.

'You could have called yesterday,' she said.

'I couldn't. I'll be back tomorrow.'

He placed the phone in its cradle, walked to the front door and opened it; it was raining. Harvey stood on the doorstep watching it fall then stepped out and stood in the middle of the lawn. He watched as a neighbour was running inside, hand in hand with her little girl. 'My wife has taken my children,' he muttered under his breath. He felt the impulse to go inside and start drinking again, but the more he thought about it the more the idea of alcohol made him feel sick. He began to walk back to the house—she was never going to come back, not Claire, not the children. He resumed standing at the door, watching the rain fall, his wet clothes dripping onto the wood floor.

The cold air made him shiver in his damp clothes but he refused to move until the locksmith arrived; it would be his penance.

'How did you manage this?' the fat locksmith asked him.

'Birthday party,' he said. 'Don't change the lock, just fix it.'

'Right,' the locksmith said, and winked. 'Don't want the missus to find out?'

'Quite.'

Once the locksmith had left, Harvey slept on the couch and woke the next morning to see Claire and the children standing in front of him.

'Are you okay?' Claire asked. She looked worried.

He nodded.

'I'm so sorry!' she said.

He sat up and looked at his family.

'It's okay,' he said. He smiled at his son and ruffled his daughter's curly hair.

'I just needed space.'

He nodded. He stood up, kissed her on the cheek and walked toward the stairs.

'Where are you going?'

He smiled and tapped his watch. 'Time to get ready for work.'

'Don't you think we should talk?'

'About what?' he asked.

Distractions

Growing up, Marge had dreamt of being an actress. Instead, she had ended up working in a bank, with three children and a husband who was rarely at home. And now it was Monday, and Marge was running late.

She had found a pair of red lace panties in her husband's jacket pocket, and the discovery stopped her from moving for some time; she sat on the edge of their double bed, staring at the underwear in her hand. When she heard her children slam the front door behind them as they left for school, she got dressed in the same clothes she had worn on Friday and put the red panties in her handbag.

It was past ten by the time she arrived at work. She walked to her partitioned area at the back of the open-plan office, switched on her computer and sat down heavily in her ergonomic chair.

'Morning.' A cheery face appeared over her partition. It was Kevin, a 27-year-old who had worked at the bank for two weeks. 'How was your weekend? Did you go out with the kids?' He picked up the framed photograph of her children, and she stiffened in her seat.

'It was fine,' she answered. She took the photograph from Kevin's hands.

'Oh man, I can't believe it's Monday. I mean, one minute you're relaxing, thinking, great it's the weekend, and then the next,' he clicked his fingers, 'you're back here again. It's depressing isn't it?' He smiled at her, showing his neat white teeth.

She looked at the photograph of her children. 'It's work.'

Kevin's head disappeared behind the partition, and she could hear him humming a tune to himself. She opened a credit card application for a Mr Bradshaw and briefly read the details.

'So—you think it's time for a coffee-break?' Kevin's head was back.

'I don't drink coffee.'

'Hey, what's up with you Marge?'

'Nothing, I'm just busy.'

He walked around the partition and held her hand as if to pull her to her feet. 'Come on, just one cup won't kill you!' His thumb stroked the top of her hand.

She looked at him for a moment and looked at his thumb stroking her pale skin. She wanted to say no, but she nodded and followed him to the staff room.

'White or black?' he asked, heaping a spoonful of instant coffee into an orange Garfield mug.

'White.'

He handed her the coffee and they sat down.

'So, are you going to tell me why you're so quiet all the time?'

'I'm busy.' She brushed a stray hair away from her forehead.

'Yeah with your children, your husband, and this place, it must be tiring?'

She took a sip of her coffee and winced as it burnt her top lip.

'Bit hot is it?' He reached over and ran his thumb over her lip.

'I'd better go back to my desk.' She stood up quickly. Her thigh knocked the table, spilling some coffee. She ignored the spreading pool and walked away.

Lying next to her husband that night, Marge replayed the moment when Kevin had touched her mouth. She decided that she would like to have an affair with him. After going through a few scenarios, she decided that he would meet her children and they would fall in love with him too. Her husband would, unfortunately, die, but his life insurance policy would make up for it. Then she and Kevin would leave the bank and the town that she had never liked, and go and live on the coast, in a house with a pool and a tennis court. They would buy a Golden Retriever and name him after her dead husband, Graham (an in-joke between the two of them) and walk him on the beach at sunset. With this final image playing in her mind, she fell into a deep sleep.

The next day she went to work wearing a trouser suit, which was a little tight around her thighs, and a pair of stilettos that she had bought for her friend's hen's party and which had caused her feet to blister painfully. She had taken the time to apply make-up and had tied her hair back into a girlish ponytail.

Kevin wasn't at his desk yet. She sat down in her ergonomic chair and turned on her computer. She smoothed down her jacket and crossed her legs. He still hadn't arrived.

She opened a credit card application and approved it, then realised that she had missed the information that the applicant was heavily in debt. If she had long nails she would have tapped them impatiently on her desk, but her nails were ragged, and Marge wasn't the type of woman to tap her fingernails anyway.

After an hour, she checked the offices in case he was with a client, then made her way into the staff room. She made herself a white coffee in the Garfield mug and sipped it, standing near the doorway. After fifteen minutes she admitted defeat, walked back to her desk and sat staring at her computer.

At one o'clock her husband called. He rarely called her at work.

'How's your day?' he asked.

'What do you want?'

'Just wondered if you wanted to go out for dinner tonight? I thought maybe Carla could babysit.'

'What for?'

'Well, to eat, I suppose.' He laughed.

She pulled the phone away from her ear a little.

'Can you give Carla a call?' he said.

'Sure. Fine. Whatever. I'll see you later.' She hung up and stared at the space where Kevin's head had been the day before.

It was after two by the time Kevin arrived. He walked into the office, stopping at Suzie's desk, a youngish mum of twins, and stood chatting with her for a while. Marge looked up as he took a pen from Suzie and put it into his shirt pocket. Suzie giggled at something he said and playfully tried to retrieve her pen. Marge looked back at her screen.

She heard him sit in his chair and turn on his computer. He sighed heavily and started to tap away at the keys. She stood up and walked past him to get a glass of water. On the way back to her desk, she looked at Kevin, who was studying his screen. He didn't look up.

Her phone rang, but she ignored it. She looked in her

handbag to find a chocolate bar, ignoring the tightness of the trousers around her thighs. She saw the red panties, put her handbag down and dialled Graham's number on her work phone.

'Hello,' he said.

'It's me.'

'What's up?'

'I can't find Carla's number so you will have to call if you want her to babysit,' she said.

'I'm a little busy Marge.'

She looked down at her handbag. The red panties seemed to be glowing in the darkness. 'I can't find it.'

He exhaled loudly. 'Fine, yes, I'll do it.'

'Okay. Thanks. 'Bye,' she said.

'Oh, and Marge?'

'What?'

'I love you. See you tonight.'

She hung up.

She took her rarely used make-up bag out of her top drawer and applied some more blush to her cheeks. She scrabbled around in the bag until she found a bright red lipstick; bits of fluff were stuck to it, and she wiped them away with a tissue. She dragged the lipstick around her thin lips, catching it slightly on her front teeth, leaving a red smudge.

At three o'clock, Kevin stood up and walked to the staff room; Marge followed.

'You were late today,' she said.

'Yeah, some staff training shit. Completely boring and pointless if you ask me.' He turned and smiled at her.

'Coffee?'

She nodded.

'Hey that's two days in a row! I must be rubbing off on you!'

She sat at the table.

'There you go. I even remembered no sugar, right?' He placed the mug in front of her. The Garfield mug.

'Well, I'd better get back to it,' he said, and walked out of the staff room.

Marge stared at the milky coffee. She took a sip and left a red lipstick smear on the rim. She wondered whose mug it was and whether they would mind a lipstick smudge on it. She poured the coffee down the sink and left the mug, unwashed, on the draining board.

As Marge got to her desk, she saw Suzie leaning over Kevin's shoulder, showing him how to link spreadsheets. Marge could see Suzie's hand on top of Kevin's as she moved the mouse around for him.

Marge opened a new email and started to type. She heard Suzie laugh at something Kevin had said, and she typed quicker. When she had finished, she pressed send, sat back in her chair and smiled.

At the end of the day, Kevin stood and walked out without saying goodbye to Marge. She waited until all her colleagues had left, then reached into her handbag and pulled out the red panties. She walked over to Kevin's desk, looked around the deserted office, then opened his top desk drawer and placed them inside. She went into the bathroom and wiped away the red lipstick. She untied her hair from its ponytail, letting it hang to her shoulders in knotty waves. Looking in the mirror she saw dark circles under her eyes and patches of dry skin appearing beneath her smears of foundation. She rubbed at the soft skin under her eyes, making them puffy. She took a pair of flat shoes out of her handbag and changed into them.

Scanning herself in the mirror she felt that she looked like her normal self again. She looked at her thighs stretching the fabric of the trousers, and at her swollen feet now ensconced in comfortable flats and felt a little foolish for trying to be the kind of woman who wore stilettoes.

Walking up three flights of stairs to the top floor made her sweat, and as she reached the top, she took off her jacket, rolled it into a ball and stuffed it into her bag.

Adrianna's office was through a pair of heavy glass doors, and she pulled at them, stumbling in.

'Oh Margaret, look at the state of you!' Adrianna hurried over and helped her into a chair. 'Can I get you some water?'

She shook her head. 'Thank you for seeing me so late.'

'Not at all. When I got your email, I didn't know what to think.' Adrianna sat in a chair close to her.

'I didn't know what to do.' Marge looked at her thighs.

'Well, don't you worry about a thing. I'll take care of everything.'

'I don't want him to know it was me.' Marge sniffed. 'It will be awkward to work with him.'

'He'll have to know it's you, Marge.'

'There's one more thing.' Marge played with her wedding band.

'Yes?'

'I think he has some sort of fetish too. He keeps these red lace panties in his top desk drawer…'

Adrianna leaned forward in her chair. 'Has he shown them to you, Marge?'

She nodded.

'Unbelievable.' Adrianna shook her head slowly.

'I can't look at him.'

Adrianna wrapped her arm around Marge's shoulder. 'I'll make sure you don't have to see him again, okay?'

Marge twirled the wedding band round on her finger again and cried.

At seven o'clock, Marge arrived at La Petite Auberge and sat across from Graham.

'Did you have a good day?' he smiled at her.

'Not bad,' she answered and smiled back. 'Can we order champagne? I'm in the mood for celebrating.'

Wasted

John stood in the kitchen, wearing just his shorts and vest, and wondered why he had bothered to wake up at six am. He switched on the kettle and stretched.

'What are you doing today?' his mother asked.

'Not sure,' he said. He spooned instant coffee into his mug. He shook his head—coffee would keep him awake, and he wanted to sleep. He emptied the coffee into the bin and searched for a tea bag.

'You could sort your room like I've asked you to? I've already told Karen that we have at least ten boxes of stuff to donate and probably all of them are yours—'

'Do we have any normal tea?'

'What?'

He held two boxes of herbal teas in his hands.

'*We* have the tea *we* drink. If *you* want "normal" tea then *you* will have to buy some.' She picked up her keys off the counter and slammed the front door behind her as she left.

He put the tea back into the cupboard, walked over to the fridge, and opened it. He stared at the shelves of food and picked up a carton of orange juice.

'I hope you're not thinking of drinking that straight out of the carton?' his dad said.

John put the orange juice back on the shelf and closed the fridge door. He watched as his dad sat at the table and spread the morning paper in front of him.

'Has your mum gone already?' he asked.

John turned away, took some bread out of the breadbin and put it into the toaster.

'Did you watch the game last night? Pathetic,' his dad said.

The toast popped up, burnt on one side. 'The toaster's broken, and you have no normal tea.'

'Tell your mother when she gets in.'

John spread butter on the toast.

'I'm off, be good,' his dad said, and play-punched him on the arm as he walked out.

John ate his toast standing at the counter and looked out of the kitchen window.

A large gum tree shaded the side of the house. When he was younger he used to sit under the shade of the sweet-scented leaves and read books. He looked now at the brown grass and red dirt of the garden and missed the cool sea air of Melbourne's coast.

He finished his toast and rinsed his plate in the sink. He walked slowly up the stairs and went into his bedroom. Empty cardboard boxes littered the floor, creating an obstacle course to his bed. He stubbed his toe on the edge of the wardrobe and swore under his breath. Then he remembered that his parents weren't home and said, 'shit,' loudly. He sat on the edge of his bed and wondered whether he should do what his mum had asked him to, and sort out his room. He looked at the action figures, lined up on a shelf, which he had collected since junior school. He stood up and put a few in a box, then took them out again and laid them back on the shelf. He would think about it for a while, he decided.

He grabbed his Walkman and earphones from his bedside table and chose some music – AC/DC would do. Then he opened the drawer of his bedside cabinet and grabbed a tin full of tobacco mixed with fragrant green shredded leaves, some papers, and his lighter, before making his way back downstairs, then outside. His last stop was the fridge in the garage, where he pulled out a six-pack of beers.

In the shade under the gum he sat down and expertly rolled a joint. Then he smoked slowly, lying on his back, at first watching the curling grey fumes disappear into the leaves above him. After a little while he closed his eyes and listened to the music.

He was halfway between being awake and sleeping when he felt something nudge his side. He opened his eyes and saw Paula, their neighbour, standing over him. He took his earphones out.

'Are you smoking pot?' she asked. 'I could smell it from my garden. It's strong.'

'Oh,' he said. He sat up.

'You're back from school then?'

'University.'

She sat down next to him, and he looked at her. She was his mother's age, but she looked younger, and she wore cooler clothes.

'Your dad said you were doing well, but he never mentioned your habit.' She laughed. 'Funny, I never would've picked you as the type.'

'Me neither,' he said.

'How old are you now? Nineteen?'

'How old are you?'

'Forty.'

'I'm twenty-one,' he lied.

'Really? I could've sworn you were a bit younger.' She scratched her head and then smoothed her long blonde hair so it fell over one shoulder. 'You're just going to sit here all day then?' She picked up his earphones and put them in her ears. 'What are you listening to?'

He turned the music back on for her.

'That's not music, it's noise!'

'That's what Dad says.'

'Yeah? Well your dad's right.'

'What do you listen to then? Sinatra?' He laughed.

'Sometimes. Depends what mood I'm in. Whatever I listen to, I always listen to an LP. Nothing like a record. All this new technology doesn't compare.'

'Prove it,' he said.

She looked at him. He blinked a few times and looked at the top of her ear and felt his face getting hotter. Then he decided her face was okay to look at, and he looked directly into her eyes.

'Okay,' she said. She stood up and held out her hand. He took it and pulled himself up. 'Don't forget your smokes and booze,' she said, nodding at the tin, 'we'll need those if we're going to listen to some serious music.' He picked them up and followed her.

He had never been in her house before, and he wondered if his parents had either. It was hot and stuffy even with all the windows open. Paula walked into the kitchen with the beers and left him in the living room.

'I don't have aircon,' she said.

Her couch was brown leather. He sat on it and liked the cool feeling on the back of his thighs. He noticed a recliner in the corner: it was like his grandma's.

She walked back into the room with two beers and a bowl of chips on a tray. She put the tray down and switched on a fan that sat on a small table next to the chair.

'That's better,' she said. She sat down and pulled the

lever at the side so that the footrest popped up. 'Are you going to roll, or shall I?'

He took a swig of his beer, ate a couple of chips and rolled a large joint. His head was still fuzzy from the one earlier, and when he looked at Paula's long brown legs poking out from her denim shorts, he thought that maybe he liked them.

'Pass it over; I'll light, and I'll let you choose the music,' she said. He handed her the joint. She pointed. 'In the corner over there.'

He walked over to the record player and flicked through the records.

'Anything you like?' she asked. He looked over his shoulder at her and saw she was lying on the recliner with her eyes closed. 'Don't worry, I've saved you some,' she said.

He turned back to the records and picked out a blues album. He turned the record player on, lifted the needle carefully and set the black disc in, lowering the needle down onto the first groove. Then he sat on the couch as Nina Simone's rich voice filled the room.

'Here.' She handed him the rest of the joint; there was only a quarter left. She lowered the footrest and grabbed a beer. Her eyes were glassy. 'I'm surprised you picked this one,' she said.

'I'm full of surprises,' he said. He smoked the rest of the joint in three heavy drags, drank some beer and rolled another.

'Good boy,' she said. 'You ever had a record player?'

'Gran had one. Dad has it now.' He wanted to tell her that his gran also had the same chair, but he didn't.

She drank her beer and watched him smoke, humming along with a bit of the song she knew well. He saw she was sweating, and now and again she scratched at her head.

'My turn,' she said. She held out her hand to take the joint from him.

He didn't think it was that hot in the room, but he saw sweat was dripping off her reddened face, and through the fog of the drug he felt worried. 'I don't think you should have anymore. I don't think it's affecting you too well,' he said.

'Oh this?' She wiped her hand across her face. 'This is nothing to do with that! Here, give me the smoke, get us some more beers and I'll tell you a secret.'

He looked at her face and didn't want to give her the joint, but he did anyway and went into the kitchen to get the drinks. As he walked, his feet felt like they were treading on cotton wool, and there was a buzzing noise in his ears. If he had been under the tree in the garden listening to his music, he thought, he would like this feeling. But right here in this kitchen, he wasn't so sure.

He walked back into the living room and gave her a beer. She looked at him for a moment with a funny smile on her face. 'Are you ready?'

He nodded.

She put the beer on the table, sat up straight, and looked at him. 'Ta da!' she shouted, and with one quick movement took all her hair off her head.

He wobbled where he stood, blinked a few times and couldn't understand where her hair had gone. Then he realised. 'Shit,' he said. He sat down and drank some of his beer, and all the time he could feel her looking at him. He glanced at her head a few more times and felt shock each time he did. He thought of a girl he knew at university, Lisa, and how she had hair like Paula's wig, and he wondered what she would look like if she were bald.

'Penny for your thoughts?' she asked. He looked at her again and tried to keep looking at her but couldn't.

'It's okay,' she said. 'Most people don't know what to say. Your parents don't know, so don't tell them okay?'

He nodded. 'Okay.'

'I don't want anyone fussing around bringing me home-cooked meals. Unless they have this,' she waved the stub of the joint about, 'they're wasting their time.'

She put the end of the joint in the ashtray and moved the fan so it blew only on her face.

He watched her and saw her hands were shaking. She tried to pull the lever for the footrest to pop up and couldn't do it. He walked over and pulled it for her. She lay down and closed her eyes. He saw that her head was like a baby's; fine blonde downy hair covered her skin so she wasn't completely bald. He wanted to run his hand over it to see if it felt as soft as it looked.

'I'll get going,' he said.

'No! Sit, sit!' She opened her eyes and looked at him. 'Finish your beers.'

He nodded at her and sat down.

'Roll one more before you go.'

'Sure,' he said. He smiled at her even though she had closed her eyes again. He looked at her bald, baby-like head and felt a bit sick. 'Shall I start?' he asked.

'Sure,' she said, but she sounded far off to him now, and he wasn't sure whether it was because she was falling asleep, or because the weed was messing with his hearing.

He took some deep drags and the sick feeling went away. He leaned back on the sofa, closed his eyes and tried to listen to the blues singer on the old record, but all he could hear was the whirr of the fan.

He smoked all of the joint this time, and she didn't ask for any. He sat with his eyes closed until the record stopped playing, then he stayed for a bit longer listening to the sound of her breathing. When he opened his eyes, the room was cooler, and he noticed that the sun had moved to the back of the house. He squinted and looked at the time; it was after four. He stood up and looked at her: she was still sleeping. He noticed she had goose bumps on her legs, so he took a blanket from the back of the couch and draped it over her. He couldn't decide whether to turn the fan off, or leave it on. In the end, he left it on; she would wake up sooner or later, he thought.

Before he left, he leaned over her to make sure she was definitely breathing and gently stroked her head.

When he got home, he made some coffee and sat for a while at the table. Then he realised how hungry he was, grabbed a loaf of bread out of the bread bin and made toast, the toaster burning one side of the bread.

He made four rounds of toast and took them up to his room. He rolled a weak joint this time, adding more tobacco, then sat next to the open window and smoked as he ate. When he had finished he sprayed air-freshener in his room until he could no longer smell the tangy scent. One by one he took the action figures off his shelves and placed them in a box. He took the posters off the walls and took the comics out of his drawers.

His mum walked into the room, and he turned and looked at her.

'Good to see you haven't wasted your day,' she said.

'The toaster's broken,' he said and turned back to his packing.

It

is

something

to

be

sure

of

a

desire

The stuffed bear sat on the mantelpiece, its black, beady eyes staring at me as I sipped bitter-tasting ice tea. The bear had company on the mantel, a blue elephant with I LOVE USA stitched into its soft belly in red, white, and blue. A stuffed rabbit, its ear chewed (presumably, hopefully, by a dog) sat in the middle of the flowery couch and looked as if it had never been moved.

Francis walked into the room, followed by Joyce and Bill, his neighbours. Although it was my first night visiting him in America, he had already arranged for me to come to a barbecue.

Joyce sat on the couch next to the rabbit and smiled widely at me. She was a large woman and wore a dress that was far too small for her, showing all her curves and a good deal of her large thighs streaked with spidery green and blue veins.

'How do you like America so far, Mr Winter?' she asked.

'Harry, please,' I said.

'Sorry. Harry.' She smiled.

'As far as I can see it's splendid.' America and its citizens seemed extremely odd to me.

Francis took the empty chair next to me, whilst Bill stood awkwardly, his big frame threatening to fill the room.

'You'll have to see the sights, won't he Bill?'

Bill looked at me and nodded.

'There are some lovely sights. Me and Bill, well, when we first came here to Hillside, we saw everything. Didn't we Bill? It's really nice. Nice for kids; lots of parks and a zoo. Do you have children Harry?'

'Yes,' I said. 'They're grown now.'

She nodded at me and looked at the stuffed rabbit. She fingered its chewed ear and I saw Bill watch her closely.

Finally he spoke to me, his eyes still on Joyce.

'So, Harry,' he said, 'you want to come out back with me and Francis and see the barbecue? Got it today especially for our honoured guest.'

'I would like that,' I said. Anything to get me away from this strange room of stuffed animals.

We walked out to Bill's garden: a sprawling lawn and haphazardly placed tubs of flowers. His giant gleaming metal barbeque sat on what Bill called the deck. I pulled up a chair and watched as he and Francis played with it to get it hot for the food.

After an hour or so, others began to arrive. First, Francis' wife, who had rushed from work, she told us, as she smoothed down her jacket and patted her hair. She introduced me to her other neighbours, a tall man who looked like money with a wife who had very little to say.

I didn't know whether it was the jet lag, or the beers that were now being given to me in quick succession, but I felt my brain freeze up. I was sick and wobbly watching the couples milling about on Bill's lawn. They didn't seem real to me; they stood too straight; held their glasses just so; they patted their spouses on their arms in a loving way, while looking at them with eyes full of disinterest. I couldn't understand it. Nor could I understand Francis and the wife he had chosen. She was too loud for him. I doubted that she ever read a book. How could Francis talk to this woman every day? What on earth did they have in common?

I scanned the mannequin couples and realised that Joyce had still not joined the party. I stood up and walked over to Bill.

'Where's Joyce?'

'Oh, she's not so good with lots of people. I expect she'll be out soon.'

'Why did you have so many over,' I asked, 'if she's not comfortable?'

Bill looked at his guests. 'It was her idea,' he said. 'She'll be out soon.' He flipped a bleeding hunk of meat on the grill.

I walked away from him, through the double doors back to the living room, shaking my head the entire time. Was it the jet lag or were these Americans particularly odd?

Joyce was still sitting on the couch, humming softly as she circled items in the newspaper with a red pen.

'Hello Joyce,' I said, startling her.

She looked at me, then down at the paper in her hand.

'It's a lovely party,' I ventured.

'Did Bill send you in here?'

'No.'

'Ah good,' she said. She folded up the newspaper and hid it underneath a cushion.

'I think I'll join you now,' she said, smiling at me. She pulled her tight dress over her thighs and plumped up her hair in the mirror, finally adding a streak of red lipstick to her thin lips.

'How do I look?'

I looked at her, all of her, and saw that once she had been a very attractive woman. Now though there was something about her, some sort of desperation seeping from her, which made me feel sorry for her.

'You look lovely,' I replied and held out my arm to escort her to the party she had wanted.

By the time the sun had started to set, the couples had lost their mannequin composure; more than likely the copious amounts of alcohol had helped loosen their tightly wound minds and stiff limbs. They now milled about, couple to couple, Francis' wife chatting to the tall man with money while his quiet wife stood off to one side with Francis. Joyce was now transformed and had found her voice, a voice which laughed and chatted happily with everyone. Bill sat on the deck next to his metal barbeque; the coals glowing and sending smoke spiralling into the air. He smiled with satisfaction at his wife, now and again leaving his post to check on her and the other guests.

My eyes were closing. The long journey here was harder than I thought it would be. I felt a hand on my shoulder and looked up to see Bill.

'You wanna go lay on the couch?'

I nodded and allowed him to help me up, his strong arm leading me to the living room. He picked up the rabbit from the couch and placed it on the coffee table. I lay down, my head sinking into the cushion. I turned to get comfortable and heard the rustle of a newspaper. I pulled it out and opened it to see what Joyce had been busy circling earlier.

The page was full of classified advertisements. Dozens of small boxes of people's profiles for dating. Ten were circled on the page. I shook my head and put the newspaper next to the chewed rabbit. I was right, Americans were odd.

Air Mail

Martin did not like flying, so he drank heavily to sleep through. After spending nine hours in economy over the Atlantic, he landed in Virginia a little drunker than he would've liked.

He took a cab to the small town of Hillside and asked the driver to take him to an American diner, like the ones he had seen on TV when he was a child. The driver took him to a giant steel restaurant that had a cherry red-and-white striped awning in front. The sign was red too, and flashed intermittently, advertising the diner to be *Jenny's*. He paid the driver and gave an extra twenty dollars as a tip. As he got out of the cab with his small tartan suitcase, he felt stupid for tipping so much and blamed it on the vodka he had drunk on the plane.

Inside the diner, Martin picked a booth near the jukebox and sat down. For a while, he watched the other diners eat stacks of pancakes and drink down endless cups of coffee, and he wondered what life would be like in Wantage if they had a diner like this on every corner.

A waitress came over to his table; her nametag said she was Pam. Pam was about forty and wore a candy-striped dress that rode up as she walked, exposing large creamy thighs.

'You ready?' she asked.

He hadn't looked at the menu, but needed to sober up. 'Coffee,' he said. 'And pancakes.'

'Sure,' she said.

He watched her walk away, pulling at her dress and

trying to stretch it further down her legs. He removed the latest letter from inside his jacket and smiled at the little love hearts dotting the i's. The thought that she was so close to him now made him feel a little giddy, although, he thought, it could still be the effects of the vodka.

Pam brought his coffee and food. 'You British?' she asked.

He nodded and ate a forkful of pancake.

'You don't look British.' She shook her head at him then walked away.

He watched Pam serve coffee to three big-armed men who sat on stools at the counter. One of them asked for her number. She pulled her dress down and told them to go to hell. They laughed as she walked away.

He felt a little better after eating and thought that maybe he was ready. He walked up to the counter and asked a teenage girl, who was lazily polishing glasses, if they had a pay phone. She looked at him and tilted her head toward the wall beyond the big armed men.

'Do you have something a little more private?' he asked quietly.

'Why?'

'Well, it's a private conversation, you know.' He spread his hands wide as if that would explain everything.

'That's the only one.'

He checked his pocket for some change and straightened himself up and walked over to the pay phone, acutely aware of the men's eyes on him as he dialled. He heard it ringing and imagined it echoing around a large airy apartment. She would be at her desk, writing furiously at her novel. Her long black hair would be spilling down her back. She would hate to be interrupted, but would stand and quickly walk to the telephone.

After ten rings, she still hadn't answered, so he hung up and walked back to his table, the men's eyes on him once again.

'You all finished?' Pam stood next to his table, one hand holding the coffee urn, the other wedged in the skin of her fleshy hip.

He checked his watch: it was just after three. He would wait. 'Another coffee?' he said. 'And maybe a burger.'

'Sure,' she said. She poured the coffee into his cup and took away his empty plate.

He tapped his fingers on the table top and watched the three big-armed men as they ate their food.

'You want fries with your burger?' Pam was back.

'Okay,' he said.

'I didn't ask before because it always comes with fries. But then I said to Ern in the kitchen that seeing as though you're British, you may not know, and he said, "Well, go ask him then."' She smiled at him and he smiled back. Then her smile dropped, and she said, 'So I'll tell Ern, fries it is.'

He shook his head a little as she left, and wondered if Ern liked British people or not and whether it was true that staff sometimes spat in your food.

He looked over at the men. They had finished their food and were asking Pam for dessert. She bent down to the fridge, and one of the men stood on the cross-strut of his footstool, leaning over the counter to look at her. He wolf-whistled and his friends laughed. She stood up and pulled at her dress, slammed the cream pie on the counter, told them to help themselves and walked through a pair of swing doors to the kitchen. Martin walked past them on his way to the phone again, and wished he had the guts to say something to them, but he knew he never would. Instead he dialled her number again, this time letting it ring out.

He slammed the phone down and rested his head against the wall, feeling a bit of jet lag and hangover start to settle on him. He heard laughter from the men behind him and, pulling himself together, made his way back to the booth where he leaned his head in his hands and half-closed his eyes.

Pam appeared with his burger, which was the size of a small football, and a large side of fries. In her other hand, she held a giant glass of Coke with ice. She put them in front of him. 'You're looking tired,' she said. 'The Coke will help. Gets me through my shifts anyway.'

He watched her walk back through the swing doors, still pulling at her dress.

He looked at the envelope of her latest letter to him, and saw the post-box number on it. Perhaps if he went to the post office they would tell him where her actual address was. Perhaps he could then just turn up on her doorstep rather than waiting for her to answer the phone. He ate slowly, thinking of her. He had wanted to surprise her, but now realised it wasn't going to happen.

Halfway through the burger he stopped eating and exhaled heavily. He loosened his belt and drank the Coke through a blue-and-white straw. Taking the Coke with him, he went back to the pay phone and tried her number and watched as the three men compared their greenish tattoos high up on their biceps.

'Hello?' a man answered.

Surprised, he choked on the Coke that he was drinking

and coughed into the phone.

'Hello?' the man said again.

'I'm sorry,' he spluttered. He moved the mouthpiece away and coughed heavily again. As he did, he saw that Pam was now stood behind the counter polishing glasses and was watching him. The three men started to laugh and Martin's face turned red. 'Hello,' he said. 'I'm sorry about that.'

'You okay?' the man said.

'Yes, yes perfectly. I was just calling to speak to Jane.'

'Jane?'

'Yes.' There was a long silence on the other end. 'Hello?'

'Yes. Sorry,' the man said.

Martin could hear him shuffling about, and he wondered if he was Jane's dad.

'What do you want with Jane?' the man asked.

'I'm a friend of hers.'

'Are you British?' The man's voice was not steady anymore, he noticed.

'Yes.'

'You calling from Britain?'

'No,' he said. 'Why?'

'Just wondered.'

'Is Jane there?'

'No. No, not at the moment. Where are you calling from then?'

'I'm in the States now. In Hillside actually,' he said, and then immediately regretted it. He heard the man breathe heavily into the phone.

'You come all this way to see Jane?'

'Yes,' he said. 'Is there a problem?'

'No,' the man said, 'no problem. I'll tell Jane you called,

but she's away and won't be back for a while.'

The combination of jet lag and hangover was making him feel a bit woozy, and he rubbed at his eyes and tried to understand what was happening. He was silent for a few seconds.

'Hello?' the man said.

'Yes. I'm here,' he said. He was angry now. 'When's Jane back? I'm happy to wait, you know.'

The man was quiet for a moment and asked, 'Where are you right now?'

'Jenny's Diner,' he said, and then felt stupid for telling him.

'I think it's best if I come and see you,' the man said hurriedly.

Martin could feel his heart beating hard in his chest, and he felt a little sick. 'That's okay,' he said, and forced a laugh. 'You don't have to do that. I'll speak to Jane later.'

'No,' the man said, 'it's better I come and talk to you first.'

He looked around the diner and saw Pam smile at him. He nodded into the phone. 'Okay,' he said.

'I'm Bruce,' the man said.

He hung up.

Pam came to his table with another large Coke as he sat down. He nodded at her and drank quickly, wondering if the three men would help him if Bruce turned out to be a psycho. He leaned his head back onto the cool leather of the booth and closed his eyes.

'You finished?' Pam asked.

'No.'

'It'll get cold. You want me to heat it up for you?'

'Fine,' he said.

A few minutes later, he heard a bell ring loudly, signalling that the door was opening. He opened his eyes, sat up straight, and watched the three men leave. He was tempted to leave with them, but then saw a man hold open the closing door and walk into the diner. He knew it was Bruce straight away.

The man was mid-fifties, tall and broad like he lifted weights often, and he wore a thick checked jacket. Martin saw him look around the diner for a moment before his eyes settled on him. Martin nodded slightly, watching him stride to his table.

The man held out a large hand. 'Bruce,' he said.

Martin took his hand and shook it; it was warm and rough to touch. Bruce sat across from him and looked at him with cloudy blue eyes.

Pam hovered near the table, the coffee urn in her hand.

'Coffee please, Pam,' Bruce said.

'Sure. How's Lynn?'

'The same.'

She poured coffee, smiled at Martin and gave him a quick wink. She walked away and stood behind the counter.

'I can see why she likes you,' Bruce said.

'Who?' he asked, confused. 'Pam?'

'Jane,' he said, smiling.

Martin smiled back.

'How did you meet? An ad right?'

'How did you know that?'

'That's how she meets all of them.' Bruce took a sip of his coffee.

'All?' he asked.

'Yes. All.'

'Who are you?' Martin felt sick again.

'Her husband,' he said.

'Right,' Martin managed to say. His tongue suddenly felt too big for his mouth, and he was dizzy.

'I'm sorry,' Bruce said. He leaned towards Martin. 'Her name's Lynn, not Jane. She's forty-eight, not twenty-eight, or whatever she told you.'

'Who is she then?'

'Just a wife.' He shrugged. 'It's complicated.'

'I don't understand.' Martin looked at the table top for a few minutes. A lonely hearts ad for a pen pal, at the back of The Telegraph, a dare on his 30th birthday.

'Come on, mate,' his friends had jeered. 'Still single and not even a bloody dog or cat to keep you company.'

He had told his friends that he had never received a reply after he had drunkenly posted his letter 18 months ago. But he had. And he was in love.

He could hear Bruce breathing but didn't look up. He raked a hand through his hair and wondered if Pam had a stash of vodka behind the counter.

'It's been over a year,' he said, quietly.

'I know.' Bruce stirred a little milk into his coffee.

'How do I know that you're not lying?' Martin suddenly asked, staring at him.

Bruce laughed loudly at first, scaring him. Tears streamed down his cheeks, and he clutched his stomach and leaned over in his seat. After a few minutes, his laughter died down to a chuckle, and he wiped the tears off his face with his large hand and said, 'I wish I was.'

'I can't believe it,' Martin said.

'Neither could I at first,' Bruce replied. 'It started innocently enough. Pen pals she called them. I never asked any questions. Not until I read a couple. Seems she's breaking hearts all over the world!' Bruce laughed again, and Martin wanted to leave.

'Why do you stay?' he asked.

'It's complicated.'

They were both silent for a few minutes. Suddenly, Bruce said, 'You know, I'm not from here originally?'

Martin shook his head.

'Texas. My mom and dad had a farm out there. A big place, full of a big family. I think that was one of the reasons Lynn fell in love with me—she wanted that, wanted to make herself a big family and take care of everyone.'

'Why did you leave?'

'Lynn was in an accident,' he said. 'It changed her and she struggled with life on the farm and with lots of people, so we moved here, just the two of us. Everyone said it would be a good change, you know?' He looked out of the window then looked back at Martin. 'Where are you going to stay tonight?'

'Not sure.'

'I can recommend a couple of places—take you to one if you like?'

Martin shook his head.

Bruce took his car keys from his pocket and played with them. Martin watched him turn the keys over and over in his large rough hand.

'I'm sorry,' Bruce eventually said. 'You're a good-looking man, you'll find someone one day. Someone young and pretty. You'll be okay.' He stood up and held out his hand, and Martin took it. He watched Bruce walk out of the diner, his shoulders slightly slumped under his checked jacket.

When Bruce had left, he waved Pam over for the bill.

'You need somewhere to stay?' she asked him, as he counted out notes into her hand.

'Sure,' he said.

She smiled at him and went behind the counter to get her bag, pulling at her dress as she walked.

Autumn

Frank looked out of his kitchen window and saw it was autumn. Burnt orange leaves covered the lawn and worm-holed apples littered the ground. He sipped his black coffee and watched Carl, his neighbour, get into his shining Audi and speed off down the street. He cursed him under his breath, 'the selfish ass': children were riding their bikes and he had barely glanced in his rear-view mirror.

'Coffee?' Marie asked him, searching for a clean mug in the dishwasher.

'Got some.'

'What are you looking at?' She poured coffee into her mug.

'Carl speeding down the street and nearly massacring the kids in the neighbourhood.'

'Don't you think you need to get the leaf blower fixed?'

'Didn't you hear me? He's going to kill someone one day, I swear it. Don't you care?' He turned to look at her.

She was seated at the kitchen table, turning the pages of Cosmopolitan. She stopped at the quiz page and picked up a pen. 'You say the same thing every day,' she said, ticking boxes, A, B, or C, 'and as yet, he has never killed anyone.'

'Hmmm.' He turned back to his view out of the window. 'I'll get the leaf blower fixed today.'

'Good. Would you say I am more of an arty person or more logical?'

'Yes. What?'

'The quiz I'm doing. Am I more arty? I think I am.'

'Yeah, I guess.' He poured the last dregs of his coffee into the kitchen sink and rinsed his cup.

'Besides darling, I know you like Carl,' she said, as she

turned to the horoscope page and read the fortunes of Gemini for that month.

'Do I?'

'Well, I'd say you do. You play poker with him every month, and you always go and watch football with him. I'd say,' she tapped the pen on the table as she read the outlook for Taurus, 'that means you like him.'

'He's okay I suppose.' Frank shrugged. 'It's his driving that's the problem.'

'I'm sure he doesn't mean any harm, darling.' She stood up and handed him her mug. 'Well, I'd better be going. I'll see you tonight.' She kissed him lightly on the cheek and wiped away the resulting lipstick smudge with her finger.

He washed her mug, left it on the draining board and then stood still, staring out of the window until he saw her pull out of the driveway. He went to his study and turned on the computer but he didn't sit down. Before the computer had loaded his desktop, he switched it off and opened the top desk drawer. He looked down at a stack of papers that had a packet of cigarettes placed squarely on top. He took one out of the packet, put it behind his ear, and then closed the drawer. He looked out of the window and saw the carpet of leaves.

'In a minute,' he said quietly.

He went upstairs and changed into a pair of washed-out Levis and an old blue cotton shirt that had its pocket torn off. He went into the walk-in closet and found his hiking boots next to Marie's red stilettos. He looked at them for a while: the Mr and Mrs Shoes. He couldn't remember the last time she had worn those heels.

He sat on the edge of the bed and put on his boots. Marie had changed in a hurry this morning and left her dressing gown strewn on the bed. He picked it up to hang on the back of the bedroom door, but before he did, he held it close to him, burying his face in the soft white towelling and inhaling her smell.

He went down the stairs slowly, looking at the framed pictures on the walls. There were none of him and Marie; she said photos were tacky. Instead, she had chosen floral pictures, each with the Latin name of the flower in italics underneath. Framed in gold leaf, they were perfectly spaced so each stair had a picture. Frank had never really looked at them before. For some reason, he stopped now on every stair, and ran his hand over each of the pictures, whispering the Latin names to himself: *Acacia*, *Aloe Succotrina*, *Biguonia Radicans*, *Ocimum*, and on the last stair, *Campanula*.

He went into the kitchen and made a fresh cup of coffee, and flicked through Marie's magazine on the kitchen table. She had taken the quiz, *Have you still got it in your 40's?* and had scored quite highly, Frank noticed. She was sexy, interesting and cultural, *a rare find*, the magazine said.

Frank opened the window a little, and a bar of cool air touched him. He took the cigarette from behind his ear and the lighter from the top of the kitchen cupboard, and lit the cigarette. He took deep drags and blew long, thick plumes of smoke out of the window. After just six drags, he had finished it. With one swallow he drank the rest of his coffee and looked at the garden. He pulled up his jeans a little and tightened his belt. Then he went into the garage and turned on the light. His Volvo four-wheeled drive took up most of the space and the gardening tools were neatly arranged on one wall like soldiers standing to attention. Frank saw a rake standing erect next to the broken leaf blower. He picked it up; he would rake the leaves, he decided. He flicked the switch and the electric garage door opened, the cold autumn air rushed in, hitting him in the face and making him shiver. He went back inside to get his coat.

By the time he walked outside, Carl had returned home. Frank stood next to an apple tree and watched him climb out of his low-slung car. Carl was tall and athletic, and watching him made Frank smile; it wasn't easy to get out of a sports car when you were six foot two.

'Frank!' Carl shouted, waving his arm in the air. Frank waved back and stopped smiling. He felt the cold metal of the rake in his hands and started to pull the leaves towards him.

'How's things? We still on for the football tomorrow?' Carl walked over to him, kicking leaves in his designer loafers.

'Yes good, thanks. What time's kick-off?'

'Two, I think.' Carl picked up a leaf and twirled it between his fingers. 'Listen, I just wanted to come over as well to say I'm sorry about your job. You know, things are hard right now for everyone, I'm sure you'll find something soon.'

Frank nodded.

'Marie told me about it last weekend. Why didn't you say anything?'

Frank shrugged. 'There wasn't much to say.' He rubbed at the stubble on his chin. 'Marie was away last weekend on some work thing.'

'Oh really,' Carl looked at the branches of the tree, 'my mistake. You know, I was thinking of getting an apple tree myself. But then I guess you end up having to clear the apples as well as the leaves.' He stopped twirling the leaf and dropped it on the ground.

'Marie usually gets the apples in and bakes pies. The rest stay here to rot.'

Carl bent down and picked up a shiny red apple, 'I'll take this one off your hands for you then,' he grinned.

'It's bruised.' Frank pointed to the other side, where a large brown patch had ruined the skin.

'I'll eat it anyway.' He bit into it. 'You know me, when it comes to food, I just can't say no!'

'I'd better get back to it,' Frank said, holding up his rake a little, 'Marie will kill me if she comes home and sees I haven't finished.'

'Women,' Carl rolled his eyes, 'I know what you mean. Gill's got a list a mile long for me to do today.' Carl chewed, watching as Frank raked the leaves. 'I've got a leaf blower you could borrow if you want? I've got to do my own first, but I could drop it round after?'

Frank didn't stop raking. 'No really, it's fine. Thanks anyway.'

Carl walked away. 'See you tomorrow at two,' he called over his shoulder.

Frank raked leaves. After ten minutes, his face was covered in a fine sweat, so he took off his thick woollen coat, and left it on the garage floor. He looked at the large Sugar Maple that dominated the garden, its brilliant orange and deep red leaves carpeting the front lawn. Four apple trees lined the driveway; their fallen yellow leaves speckled the neat flowerbeds. He needed the leaf blower, he knew, but he liked the feeling of his arm muscles burning with each stroke of the rake, and the pain of blisters forming on his soft hands. Using long arm movements, he raked the leaves towards him. Then he took a step to the left, followed by a long pull, the teeth of the rake rustling the leaves and pulling at the soft grass underneath. Turn—a step left. The rake snagged on a tree root, ruining his rhythm. He muttered under his breath, and started again, this time missing the root. He moved methodically along the edge of the drive, pulling the leaves into an ever-growing pile. Then he moved to the edge of the flowerbeds repeating his rhythm.

He finished the first mound and stepped back to look at his handiwork. The pile was haphazardly built, wider than it was tall; it spilled across the grass and didn't look much like a pile of leaves should. He would do better with the next one, he decided.

With his second attempt he amassed a bigger pile. His forearms burned from the effort, but when he stopped, he was happy.

He rolled up his shirtsleeves and wiped the sweat from his brow with the back of his hand, and began raking again. He heard the sound of a leaf blower start up but didn't raise his head. He found a quicker rhythm with the rake and kept with it.

His stomach rumbled, and his mouth was dry, so he stopped and checked the time—it was already midday. He looked over and saw Carl walking from the side of the house towards the front garden, carrying his red leaf blower.

'Done the back already,' Carl shouted, 'you sure you don't want it?' He didn't answer.

Carl started the leaf blower. The sound was like a vacuum cleaner, droning in Frank's ears as he worked. His forearms were beginning to tire and his shoulders hurt but he carried on, the noise from across the street spurring him to work faster.

Before he had finished the pile, the noise stopped, and

Frank stopped too. He straightened his back and groaned with the effort. He saw Carl scooping armfuls of leaves into a large green plastic bag. His wife, Gill, stood on the doorstep holding a steaming mug. He watched him drop the bag and walk to the doorstep. They sat together, side-by-side, sipping their hot drinks, chatting and smiling.

Frank got back to work, this time noticing every twinge of muscle, every pang of pain shooting through his spine. His face dripped with sweat as he worked, and if there hadn't been children living on the street, he would have taken off his shirt to feel the cool air on his back.

He licked his dry lips and concentrated on the rhythm of shifting the leaves into a pile, his eyes blurring with the mixture of red, orange, and yellow. He heard Carl resume work. He pulled the rake towards him; his aching arms moved faster, his quickening breath hanging like smoke in the cold air.

When he had finished, he stopped and looked over at Carl, who was still working. Frank smiled and walked towards the garage.

'You having a break?' Carl called, 'I'll come over in a minute, help you clear those leaves into some bags.'

'No need,' Frank shouted. He walked into the garage and found a small bottle of lighter fluid in an old cardboard box. He walked outside.

'I'll come over in just a minute,' Carl repeated. Frank shook his head.

Frank walked to each mountain of leaves and poured a few drops of liquid onto them, and pulled out his cigarette lighter. Then he bent down and ran his thumb against the wheel, and pressed down quickly on the button to release the gas.

The flames leapt over the dry leaves within seconds, creating a roaring bonfire. He walked to the other piles and lit them. Then he stood back and watched as the fires grew, sending thick columns of black smoke into the clear blue sky.

It

is

something

to

have

smelt

the

mystic

rose

The whitewashed walls were dotted with small drops of blood. I sat on the orange plastic chair next to the bed whilst Philip stood outside berating the young nurse. I held Eva's hand and tried not to look at the thick white bandage around her wrist.

She slept with her face tilted toward me. Her bald head was exposed and a thick red scar ran across her skull where they had tried to remove the ghastly tumour that was spreading its octopus-like tentacles through her brain.

I was supposed to die first. In a few more years I would be dust and she was meant to scatter me across my garden. I was not meant to do it for her, and I wasn't sure that I could.

Her blue eyes opened slowly, cloudy from the tranquilizer.

'Oh Eva,' I said.

'I'm sorry.' Her voice was rough.

'Water?'

I held the straw to her cracked lips and she sucked slowly until she was exhausted from the effort. She lay back on her pillow and stared at the ceiling.

'It hurts, Harry,' she said.

'I know.'

'You don't.'

'I know I don't Eva, but what else can I say?' I grabbed her hand again.

'It hurts me every day to watch you and Philip go through this. To hear me scream and talk nonsense.'

'We don't mind Eva, we want to take care of you. You'll get better, you'll see.'

'*I* mind, Harry.' She turned to look at me, her eyes filled with tears. 'I mind that when Francis comes to visit, sometimes I don't know who he is. Sometimes I swear at him. My own son, Harry. Swearing at my son.' She sobbed.

I didn't know what to say. For the first time in my life words failed to materialise in my brain. Sentences seemed pointless.

She fell back to sleep for a while and I watched her. Her failed attempt today to end her pain would not be her last. No matter how much Philip screamed at the nurse, no matter how much he sat by her bedside, she would find a way to go: I knew my sister.

'Harry,' she whispered. She still had her eyes closed.

'Yes?'

'I have something to tell you, but please don't hate me.'

'I could never hate you.' I smiled at her.

'Mary never died.'

I looked at her, my smile becoming fixed and hard. Was she lucid?

'She did, Eva. Remember, two days before our wedding. You sent the telegram to the barracks to tell me she died. Don't you remember?' I squeezed her hand a little harder than normal.

'I lied, Harry. She asked me to lie to you.'

I laughed involuntarily, then let go of her hand.

'I'll go and get Philip,' I said. 'You need some medicine.' I stood up out of that godawful orange chair and made for the door.

'Harry don't!' Her voice was firm. 'I'm completely lucid and you need to hear this before I go.'

I turned around slowly, feeling my stomach flip and my knees wobble.

'Come here, please.' She waved her thin hand at me. I sat on the edge of her bed and tried to breathe.

'She was pregnant, did you know that?'

I shook my head.

'She went to her aunt, but before she did she came to see me and asked me to tell you that she was dead.'

I laughed loudly now. 'That's crazy,' I said, 'really Eva, crazy. Why would she do that? Why wouldn't she just marry me?'

'Because Harry, she didn't know if the baby was yours.'

I stopped laughing. 'Who else's would it be?'

'I don't know,' she said quietly. 'She wouldn't say. She seemed broken somehow Harry. I'd never seen her like that before. She said it would spare everyone the heartache. I'm sorry but I had to agree with her.'

'Agree with her!' I shouted. 'How could you do this? Why didn't you tell me?'

'I couldn't Harry! You were going to war and I didn't know if you were coming back, or if my own husband would return. I knew if you knew the truth, it would break you.'

'What? And you didn't think that thinking she was dead would break me? Who was it, Eva? Who did she sleep with?'

'I don't know,' she said again. But I noticed that she would not look me in the eye as she spoke. It was then I began to suspect—it was like remembering, as though I had always known something deep down.

'At least you left thinking she loved you, and only you, and that's all she wanted, and all I would ever have wanted too, if I was in that position.'

I sat back in the plastic chair and Eva reached for my hand. But I didn't take it.

'Harry,' she said quietly, 'I've always hated what I did,

but I really did think it was for your own good at the time.'

'You could have told me when I returned.'

'It was too late then Harry. I was broken too. I didn't know the time of day half the time and I had a son to look after. Selfishly I knew I needed you, and I knew if I told you, you may leave me too.'

'I would never have left you,' I said, but suddenly I wasn't sure this was true.

We sat in silence and my mind traced back throughout the years. All that time I had thought she was gone, but she could have been next to me in the shop, sitting next to me on the bus.

'I saw the daughter, her daughter. Your daughter,' she said.

'Mine?'

'She looked exactly like you. I knew it was her.'

'When did this happen? Did you speak to her?'

'About a month ago. Philip and I were at the clinic and she sat down across from me. I had to. I had to know. She knew everything.'

There was a silence.

'Her name is Alison. You have two grandchildren Harry,' she said, hopefully.

'Well, you had quite the family reunion.'

'It wasn't like that.'

I tried to stay silent again but I couldn't hold out for long. 'And Mary?' I asked.

'She's still alive. She lives in Bristol.'

I nodded.

'What else did she say?' I asked.

'Who?' Eva looked at me. She was tired now.

'Alison. My daughter.'

'I can't really remember Harry. She talked about her own daughter; something about splitting up from her husband, and her son who is having a hard time with his wife too. That's why she was at the clinic – his wife was getting treatment too. I don't know if she said anything else. It was hard to follow, you know, we didn't know any of them, so... ask Philip, he'll remember.'

'Did she say she wanted to meet me?'

'Who?' she asked again.

'Alison, my daughter,' I said slowly.

Eva's eyes struggled to focus on me. 'You have a daughter Harry?' she said. 'How wonderful! Where is she? Can I see her?'

Eva was gone. Her eyes began to close as Philip walked into the room. He held his wife's hand and talked to her, but she did not respond. I stood up, opened the door and turned to look at her. I wanted to tell her that I forgave her, but I couldn't just yet.

I didn't realise that I wouldn't get another chance.

Although

it

break

and

leave

the

thorny

rods

I think I had known all these years; something had niggled at me, like a maggot eating the flesh of the dead. I had known, hadn't I? Still, it wasn't enough for me to live with what I thought I knew, I had to see Philip and find out the truth.

I didn't ask Philip right away, instead I did what we all do I suppose, and waited until Philip and I were sat in his study in the aftermath of my sister's wake, staring at the photograph of her on top of the piano.

I had drunk too much and the question to Philip did not come out of my mouth as tactfully as I had intended. Instead a torrent of nonsense: sentences of anger, hurt and grief mixed together with the alcohol.

'It was Glynn I expect? That bastard. Eva should have known better than to marry him. With Mary! Can you imagine? Really Philip can you? I'm right you know. I know I am. I always knew I think. But then I thought she died. Believed that one didn't I? What a fool I am. But yes, definitely thought before she died, "her and Glynn". There had always been that spark you know; the twinkle in Glynn's eye whenever he saw my Mary. Although he had the twinkle for Eva. For all women no doubt about it! I am right aren't I? The two of them!' I slammed the glass down on the table, spilling whisky. I looked at the liquid pooling on the polished wood and wanted to cry but the tears would not come.

'She told you then?' Philip asked, his voice barely above a whisper.

'No,' I replied. 'You just did.'

Philip nodded and sipped at his whisky, numb to it all, he had just lost Eva after all. I stared at him, feeling sick to my stomach; I had been right, I had known, my Mary and

Eva's husband Glynn.

Philip and I sat silently staring at Eva's picture again and I wondered then if Eva had lied to protect herself from ever having to see Mary again. But I realised that my sister could never be so harsh to me or even to Mary. She had carried on and played out the game to save everyone from hurt, the hurt she carried round for all of us for years.

I wondered whether if one carries that amount of pain, it causes something to grow within you? The tumour that rested on my poor sister's brain: was that my fault? Was that the pain I was meant to bear? Of knowing that Mary was alive and had betrayed me? Or, was it Mary and Glynn's guilt that ate away Eva's mind? Bit-by-bit, the guilt turning into cancerous cells, multiplying and joining with more created from pain and hurt, gradually spreading out like tentacles, making her spew vile words, then dancing in front of her eyes so that she would imagine that people were watching her, following her, laughing at her. Soon it took away her legs, turning them into useless lumps that reminded her of the days running in sunflower fields, reminding her that there wasn't much time left.

I stood and picked up my sister's photograph, her face turned just slightly from the camera so you could not see her eyes looking at you. Instead they were looking at something far off in the distance.

I didn't do enough for her.

I failed her.

And she failed me.

La Douleur Exquise

She asked me before I had even sat down. 'So,' she raised an eyebrow, 'did he call?'

'No,' I said. She knew he hadn't, but she had to ask anyway. With that voice. In that tone. Mothers: they know how to piss you off.

'Why? I mean, he said he would?'

I picked up a menu. 'I think I'll get the fish.'

'Are you not getting enough vitamins?'

'Plenty, thank you for asking Alison,' I said with a sigh.

'Don't be clever,' she said. She hated it when I called her by her name. I smiled behind my menu, feeling I had achieved a small victory of sorts.

'So, why didn't he call? After everything that's happened you would think he would at least give you some reason why? I mean—' The waiter appeared. 'She'll have the fish,' she told him, 'I'll get the salad.'

I watched the waiter walk away, wondering if he was married and whether he had to work long shifts and whether his wife would miss him.

'You know, Dad says it's fine if you move back home. You don't have to stay at Rachel's. You should come home, where we can look after you.'

I should've ordered the steak; the fish wouldn't fill me. Maybe I could order a dessert, or grab a burger on the way back to the flat.

'You know, it's hard for everyone these days.' Mum fingered the pearls at her neck. 'There's no shame in coming home.'

I looked at her as she spoke to me but I noticed she wasn't looking at me properly. Her eyes focused in on an old man at a table behind me. It was as if she was asking him to come home.

'Mum,' I said, snapping her out of it.

'So,' she said brightly. 'Will you come home?'

The waiter came back with water. 'Can I have a gin please?' I asked him and Mum at the same time. He looked at her for confirmation. She nodded.

'It won't help,' she said.

My gin arrived as her mobile rang. She went to the reception area to answer, and I looked at my gin and wished I had asked for a double.

'Your father,' she said accusingly when she returned. 'He needs me to get home right away. The Pearsons are coming over apparently, and he says he told me on Tuesday about it, but I swear he didn't!' Her face was red; she hated being caught out. Dad would get it when she got home.

'Say hi to him for me,' I said.

'You'll be okay?' She picked up her bag and coat and put a couple of twenty pound notes on the table. 'For dinner,' she said. She began to walk away then turned back, leaning down to kiss my cheek lightly.

'Thanks Mum.'

She squeezed my hand. 'You know, I can't believe it's happened again. Men. I don't understand them you know, none of them can be trusted. Just ask your Grandmother!'

With that she turned quickly and walked out, leaving a trail of sickly sweet perfume hanging in the air.

I waited a moment wondering what wisdom my 80-year-old grandmother could possibly impart, then told the waiter to cancel the order, took the money and left.

The street was crowded with people making their way home after work. With their heads bent and hands stuck deep into pockets, they elbowed and jostled their way against one another, avoiding all eye contact. I waited a moment outside the restaurant to see a gap in the crowd that I could fit into, and then stepped out, joining the masses. It was cold, and everyone had remembered to wear woollen things that would protect them. I hadn't, and my hands were red within seconds; my face stung. As I walked, I watched the pavement and played a game with myself to try to miss the cracks. I told myself if I stepped on a crack then bad things would happen. Then I remembered that they already had.

Still, I managed to miss most of the cracks, all the splodges of discoloured chewing gum, and an old Big Issue that scuttered across the pavement under the fast-moving feet.

At a pedestrian crossing, I looked up hoping to see that the night had finally settled in, but the sky was still filled with low-slung grey clouds, making the buildings seem dirty and abandoned. Through the murky light, I saw the white welcoming sign of a supermarket. I crossed the road with my head held high and navigated my exit from the human traffic into the warmth of the shop.

I went straight to the meat section where a few grey pieces of steak looked at me from their cellophane wrappers. I picked one up and prodded it with my finger.

'You're not supposed to do that,' a male voice said from behind me.

I turned around to see that the person that the voice belonged to was good looking. 'I'm probably going to buy it,' I said.

'You shouldn't. It's grey.' He prodded it with his finger.

'I felt like steak.'

'That's not steak… this is steak!' The meat he pulled out of his basket was cut thick and red.

'I got it cut over there.' He nodded at the counter where a butcher was chopping large pieces of meat.

'I'll have to get some.'

He smiled. 'You could share mine.'

I looked at the other stuff in his basket: a mango, a box of Maltesers, Pringles – friendly food. 'Okay I will,' I said.

He looked shocked, and I liked it; it gave me a funny twinge in my stomach that I hadn't felt before. It was good to feel something again.

He was giving me a once over, head-to-toe, lingering a little on my breasts.

'Okay,' he said.

He paid quickly and ushered me outside back onto the crowded pavement, gently placing his hand on my lower back so he wouldn't lose me. We didn't talk.

He didn't live far from the supermarket. Two streets away in a posh townhouse that I would never be able to afford.

'The kitchen's downstairs in the basement. The bedroom's upstairs,' he said, as he opened the front door.

My choice. 'Kitchen sounds good.'

He cooked the steak and made oven chips – cheap, easy.

I sat at the breakfast bar, made of black marble, as big as the couch I slept on at Rachel's.

There was a dining room upstairs, he told me. 'It's a bit formal,' he said.

'This will do.'

He put the plate down, and he sat across from me,

covering his food in ketchup. I shook my head.

'You don't like ketchup?'

'No.'

I ate quickly, shovelling the food into my mouth, barely looking up from my plate. He ate slower and told me things between mouthfuls: his name, Adam, his age, thirty-five; his occupation, investment banker.

'And you?'

'Emma,' I said.

'Job?' He cleaned his plate with his last chip.

'I have one.' I looked at my empty plate. I wanted more steak.

'Where do you live?'

'Do you want to show me the bedroom now?'

He cleared the plates and led me up two flights of stairs. He stopped at the top. 'I don't usually do this.'

'What?'

'Pick someone up at the supermarket.' He ran his hand through his hair. There were a few grey strands. I was going off him already.

'It's fine. I don't either. It's just, you know, one of those things.'

'Yeah but maybe we should chat or something for a while?'

There was a stair between us. I stepped up and kissed him hard on the mouth. He tasted of ketchup. I didn't like it.

'It's this way.' He took my hand and led me to a bedroom at the end of the hallway.

His bedroom was nice; nearly as nice as mine used to be. White linen, cream painted walls covered in large black-and-white photographs, and there was none of the usual mess of clothes strewn on the floor. I sat on the edge of his bed. He sat next to me.

'You're so beautiful.' He stroked my hair.

I didn't like it. I turned my face to his and kissed him again.

'Whoa, slow down. Let me look at you for a second.' He lay me down on the bed and looked at me. He kissed my stomach, pulling my top away from my skin.

I stared above me. The ceiling was nice. He had installed little spotlights that could be dimmed. I felt him remove my jeans and underwear, and then he climbed on top of me and kissed me. I closed my eyes, still seeing the warm white glow of the spotlights behind my eyelids.

He lay next to me after. He was nicer naked than with clothes on. I ran my hand over his stomach.

'A hundred and fifty sit-ups a day,' he said, smiling.

I took my hand away and looked at the spotlights again. 'I like them.' I pointed to the ceiling.

'Yeah they're great. Cost me a bomb to install!' He rolled onto his side and looked at me. I closed my eyes.

'You tired?' He ran his thumb over my eyebrows, my eyelids, and my lips. I didn't like it.

'Hmm, yeah, I'd better be off.' I sat up.

'You can stay.' He grabbed my arm.

I looked over my shoulder at him. For some reason, he had seemed better looking in the supermarket. Now, he looked waxy, plastic almost—like a Ken doll.

'I need to go.' I gently pulled my arm away and got dressed.

'Can I call you?'

I looked at him. He had wrapped a sheet around his bottom half. I was glad of that. 'I don't have a phone at the moment,' I said.

'I've never heard that line before!' he laughed. 'Seriously, what's your number? We could do this again?' He sounded like a teenager.

'Seriously. No phone. Thanks for the steak,' I gave him a peck on the cheek.

'Seriously?'

I smiled, turned, and left. I knew he was watching me but I didn't turn around and walked quickly down the stairs to the front door.

Thankfully, the clouds were gone when I stepped outside, and the inky black sky settled me. I turned left towards the flat and walked slowly, watching my breath cloud like smoke in front of me. For a moment I forgot everything, then I remembered and wondered if he had called.

Tuesdays

The bar was busy for a Tuesday. People spilled out of the front door onto the pavement, smoking cigarettes and sipping at cheap house wines and two-for-one beers.

Paul Davies navigated the crowd, sidestepping the drunken girl who was sat on the floor, legs spread, nudging past the couple who blocked the doorway with their fumbling embrace.

He made it inside and breathed heavily, inhaling the scent of stale beer that he found so comforting. The bar was dimly lit, hiding the cracks in the plastered walls and the peeling paint on the woodwork. Tatty red leather booths lined the right wall, and opposite stood a long wooden bar, lined with stools. At the far end, an empty dance floor was dotted with lights from a large disco ball hanging above. Paul watched the ball turning for a moment then looked at the bar. There were no stools free. He waited to see if someone would leave and listened to the clamour of voices drowning out the 90's playlist. After a few minutes, three people left the bar, vacating three stools. He quickly walked towards them.

Jason was serving behind the bar, chatting to a forty-something bottle-blonde whose cleavage was getting most of his attention.

'Hey!' Paul shouted to him.

Jason looked away from the fake-tanned duo and bent down to the fridge. 'Stella?' he asked.

'Is it still beer of the month?'

'Yeah.'

'In that case, I'll take two.' Paul pulled a bar stool out and sat down.

Jason placed the two bottles in front of him and poured some nuts from a large bag into an empty bowl. Paul nodded his thanks and scooped a handful out of the bowl.

A group of suited office workers stood behind him, egging on their co-worker to down a shot. He listened to their conversation, eating the nuts between swigs of his beer.

'So, to sound clichéd, do you come here often?' The bottle-blonde had turned her attention to him.

'Nope,' Paul answered.

'You sure? I'm sure I've seen you around.'

'Maybe you have.' He swigged his beer.

'Do you have children?' She moved down towards him, sitting two bar stools away. He took another gulp.

'Two.'

'They go to school around here?'

'Yep.'

'I knew it!' She clapped her hands together. 'You know, I never forget a face, and I thought I knew you as soon as you walked in. I've seen you before at Parkside, dropping your kids off. You drive a blue Range Rover right?'

He nodded.

'I'm Tanya.' She held out a heavily ringed hand.

He sighed, turned to her and took her hand lightly. 'Paul,' he said.

'You want a beer? Hey Jason, get my friend Paul here another drink, and for me, a Chardonnay. Large.'

Paul smiled at her and loosened his tie.

'You married?' She moved up another stool.

'Yes. You?'

'I was, well, technically still am.' She winked at him. 'But you know how things get. Me and Tony, well, we're sort of separated, you know? We live our own lives.'

'Tanya and Tony.' He laughed lightly under his breath and finished the rest of his bottle. He started on the next.

Tanya raised her eyebrow at him. It was drawn on.

'So you have a pass for tonight then?'

'A pass?' He couldn't stop looking at her eyebrows. Why did women do that, he wondered? Pluck all the eyebrow hair away and then draw it on.

'You know. A pass. When your wife, or girlfriend or whatever says you can go out, drink beer and come home late, even though it's a school night.'

'Yeah, I suppose,' he said. Her left eyebrow was shorter than the right he noticed. He wanted to reach over and rub away some of the longer one, then he might stop looking at them.

'It's hard isn't it when you've got children? I've got three of them, but I'm lucky they're nearly grown up so it gives me time to get away for a bit.'

'How old?' he asked.

'Youngest is twelve, almost a teenager. The other two are fourteen and sixteen. I keep telling them that soon it will be their turn to look after me!' she laughed loudly. He could see her back fillings were gold capped. 'So, how late are you allowed to stay out for?' She moved to the stool next to him.

Jason placed a new bottle of Stella in front of him, and he wiped the condensation off it with his thumb.

'I'm going home soon,' he said.

'You don't have to you know. You could stay here and keep me company.'

'It's okay. Thanks.' He stood up and drank the rest of his beer in one. He picked up the new bottle and walked out of the bar.

'What's your problem?' she shouted after him.

No-one was outside. The smokers had gone back in, and the kissing couple had probably gone home, he decided, to take the embrace further.

He turned right, following the road until it reached the park. He walked through the black iron gates towards the playground, sat on a red swing, and took a swig of his beer. His mobile phone vibrated in his pocket. He took it out and looked at the screen. Home was calling him.

'Hello.'

'Dad it's me.' His seven-year-old son Jamie, sounded serious. 'When are you coming home?'

'I'm on my way.' He heard a shuffling noise on the other end, then a slam of a door.

'Dad,' Jamie whispered, 'I think you should come home now.'

'What's the matter?' Paul was suddenly alert.

'Mum's gone to bed. She says she's sick, and Anna won't make me any dinner because she said you told her she can't use the oven. And I asked Mum, and she sounds all funny again, and I don't know what she means.' Jamie cried. Big sobs and hiccups followed.

'I'm coming now son,' he said. 'Where's Julia? Put her on the phone, and I'll get her to start your dinner.'

'Julia went home.'

'Home? She's meant to stay until I get back!' He jumped off the swing and threw the bottle on the ground.

'Mum told her to go away and said swear words and everything. And Julia cried and said she didn't want to come back.'

'It's okay. It's going to be okay,' he told his son breathlessly, as he half-ran out of the park towards the high street. 'I'm sorry. I'll be home really soon okay? Just go and sit with Anna, and I will order us a pizza when I get in.'

'With pepperoni?' Jamie sniffed.

'With pepperoni,' Paul repeated.

'And extra cheese?' He could hear Jamie scuffling about again.

'And stuffed crust.'

'Okay then.' Jamie hung up.

He stopped at the empty taxi rank and leaned against a lamppost to catch his breath. He put the phone in his pocket. One night a week, that's all he asked for, he thought. He would have to call Julia and see what he could do to entice her back. If she quit on him for good he doubted he would get anyone else. Julia was number nine; the agency would probably blacklist him. He rubbed a hand over his face trying to wipe away the tiredness.

'You want to share?' a woman's voice behind him asked. He turned and saw Tanya walking towards him.

'Don't worry, I won't try it on with you again.' She winked at him, 'You look tired, you okay?'

'Long day,' he said.

'So, you want to share?'

'Depends where you live.' He watched her as she buttoned up her coat over her goose-pimpled skin.

'I live in Westbury.'

He raised an eyebrow.

'What? Do you think I'm not classy enough to live in Westbury? Tony's a lawyer I'll have you know.'

'No, no not at all,' he shook his head. 'I'm in Westbury

too. Bampton Lane.'

'Great, we'll share then.' She delved into the giant red handbag she was carrying, pulled out a lipstick and walked over to a shop window to apply a pink smear to her lips.

'You know, I never see your wife about anymore.' She fussed with her hair and admired her reflection. 'She used to drop your kids off a fair bit.'

'How do you know my wife?'

'I know your kids. Jamie and Anna. I told you in the bar I recognised you from dropping your kids off. Anna was in the orchestra two years ago with Donna. Your wife, never met her. Just saw her. Pretty woman.'

'She's sick,' he said.

She turned back to face him, her eyes wide in surprise, her eyebrows raised; the left one was now smudged, he noticed.

'No-one really knows,' he said.

She walked a few steps closer to him.

'It's hard,' he said.

A taxi pulled into the rank; she took him by the elbow and opened the door for him. He got in and laid his head back on the headrest as she got in the other side.

'Where to?' the driver asked, without turning round.

'Bampton Lane,' she answered, and took Paul's hand as the taxi pulled away.

He turned his head, looked out of the window and watched as the concrete of the city gave way to the green trees and lawns of suburban life. Warm glows of lights shone out of houses as families sat down to eat. He needed to go shopping, he realised; there was barely any food in the house.

He looked over at her. She winked and squeezed his hand.

'You okay?'

He leaned over and kissed her softly on the lips. The sticky pink lipstick tasted strange, he thought.

'What number?' The taxi driver was slowing down. Paul pulled away from her.

'Number 25.' He pulled his wallet out of his back pocket and handed her the money.

'This one's on me,' she grinned at him, 'Tony can afford it.'

'Thank you.' He smiled at her.

She leaned over and wiped the lipstick off his lips as the taxi pulled up to the kerb. 'Maybe see you next week,' she said.

He climbed out of the car and closed the door.

It

is

something

to

have

watched

whilst

all

have

slept

It was May and my son, Thomas, visited to see if I was dead yet. He sat across from me, looking like his mother Barbara, and was as vile as she had been toward the end.

I assured him I was fine after my fall. He wanted me to go into a home, but I dismissed him with a flick of my wrist and ignored him as he blathered on about safety and old age.

At four he left, and I picked up the magazine I had been reading before he had disturbed me. The magazine had fallen through the letter box that morning, and was something I would normally ignore—its pages advertised holidays for the aged, and various things around the home that would aid my failing body. But on the front cover was a photograph of the SS Great Britain that was moored in Bristol. I didn't care for the ship, but Bristol called to me as it had years ago when I had learned that Mary was still alive.

After Eva's funeral I had decided that to try and see Mary—or my daughter—was pointless. To dig up the past would not erase all those years. Eva had done this for my own good, and perhaps she had been right to do it.

There was no doubt that the years were now coming to an end. My writing career, whilst 'illustrious', was slowing bit-by-bit. My novels took longer to write and I found I had no pride in them anymore. Collectively they were about lives I had known, but never lived. And what life then, had I really lived? A mismatch of good sentences and sloppy characters, plot points and pathetic story lines. Was that my life's work? Was that how everyone would sum me up? Was that my life?

The collections of short stories bound into diaries were

the only things I felt were truly real and showed lives as I had understood them. But I could never publish them, they were too much of me. So I wrote still, hoping that a novel would come out of me that I could be proud of, that I could say I had spent my whole life writing.

I looked at the magazine in my lap. There it was in black-and-white: a day trip to Bristol, another chance to see my past—to see the life I could have had. Without thinking too much, I called the number and booked it; I wouldn't see her, I told myself; I would just look at the ship.

The morning started out cold and on my arrival in Bristol the wind picked up and turned the cold into something more personal. It slammed into my body, so I wrapped my coat around me tightly and donned a Russian bearskin hat; I was too old for this, I knew.

Almost straight away I made my escape from the tour and wandered the streets without any particular place in mind. Each older woman I saw, I wondered if it was her; I wondered, would she recognise me now? Was that her in the red coat at the bus stop? Or was she the one with a small dog chatting to someone outside the post office?

I realised that I was driving myself insane. I should not have come here. I made my way back toward the harbour, found a café and ordered a cup of tea. As I stirred a sugar into my cup, I could almost hear her voice from when we were young, telling me she was too sweet for sugar in her tea. I had kissed her and told her I agreed. The memory made me smile for a moment until I began to wonder whether she had shared jokes and sweet kisses with Glynn. Had they been in love?

I shook the thought away. As Eva had said, it was better

to go away believing that I was the only person she had ever loved. Then I remembered sitting with Eva, saying goodbye.

By four o'clock I re-joined the last leg of the tour, a boat trip for an hour. I boarded the ship and stood at the railing whilst the others shielded themselves inside from the cold. I watched the shoreline, knowing that she would not be there but continuing to stare anyway. I squinted until the buildings, the people, and the shoreline became dots and dashes, sending out hopeless messages as I had once done, and finally once more I was left with the gloomy waves rolling one on top of the other.

****

One month later I knocked on Philip's front door and realised that I had never before felt such nervousness at seeing him. He opened the door and didn't greet me, but instead turned and walked toward his study: this didn't bode well.

He sat behind his desk and clasped his hands.

'You read it?' I asked.

'You said you never saw Mary,' he answered.

'I didn't.'

'So why do you write of her?' Philip held my manuscript in his hand and thumped it onto the desk in front of him. 'And Francis told you about what was going on with his life over there too? A wife cheating with their neighbour?' He jabbed his finger into the front page, creasing it.

I shook my head.

'And Eva? You write of her as if you were there, as if you saw it all.' he shouted. 'How could you Harry?'

I sat in an armchair and looked at my friend—although he didn't look like someone I knew anymore.

'It's real,' I said at last. 'Don't you see Philip, this is what I have been waiting my whole life to write. It's good, isn't it?'

Philip stared at me. 'It's good Harry. It's your best work. But it'll never sell.'

'Why not?' I asked.

Philip just shook his head.

'If you won't publish it I'll find someone who will.'

The clock on the mantelpiece marked the time as we sat in silence staring at one another: two old men, too old to fight, but still with the will to win. We were left with that kind of sour-faced stubbornness the old sometimes have.

'I'll read it again,' he said. 'Give me some time with it. But think about who this is going to hurt.'

I waved my hand dismissively. 'They're just stories, Philip. Stories from an old writer.'

'They are too alike to the people we know and love, Harry. They're other people's stories. Surely you must see that?'

'They're fictional,' I said. 'I used my creative licence. We wouldn't be sued, if that's what you are worried about?'

'Harry, I ask you to do me this favour, that if I read this again and feel I cannot sell this, then you must trust me on this. Can I please ask you to do this for me? Will you promise me that?'

I looked around his study, my eyes settling on the framed photograph of Eva and Philip on their wedding day.

'I promise,' I said.

Mary

They don't understand, none of them do, what it's like to be old. They would rather see me in a home: locked away where I can't fall and make a fool of myself—or of them.

That was why, when I saw him today, I held onto my shopping cart, my knuckles turning white, so I wouldn't fall. The wide high street offered no buffer against the strong wind blowing in from the north, and I stood there, gently swaying as the wind pushed against me.

He was at the bus stop, waiting to catch the 49 that runs up to the church on the hill, then round to the posh houses that have a view of the town, looking as if he belonged—as if he had every right to be standing there, in Bristol. He hadn't of course, but with his grey wool coat wrapped around him, his beret placed jauntily at an angle on his head, he was just how I remembered him, and I almost believed for a second that he had been there all this time and that somehow my old eyes had failed to see him.

I wanted to shout his name, but the cold wind took my breath away from me, taking with it the years I had waited for this moment. The 49 rounded the corner, and he began to shuffle forward in the queue, his eyes trained on the arrival of the bus, now and again flitting down to the ticket in his hand. I watched him board, my brain telling my paralysed body to move and to shout. It was only after the bus had pulled away that I found I could even think again, let alone move. He always had that power over me: the mere thought of him could make my legs turn to jelly and my mind freeze.

I did the rest of my shopping in a daze. His face after all these years hadn't changed. I knew it wouldn't have, he's just annoying like that; while the rest of us age and sag he just wills himself to be the same: still handsome, still charming—

I bought a pineapple. Not the time of year for pineapples really, but that's the way the world is now, you can buy a pineapple in December and strawberries in January. I wasn't sure why I bought the pineapple, maybe seeing him again had sent me funny in the head. Still, I paid for it, £1.50, for a pineapple that I knew would now sit in the fruit bowl and silently mock me for the old fool that I was.

I got home just as Iris next door was letting her cat out. I stopped to chat, not really wanting to hear her babble, but I did it anyway, because that's what you do isn't it, when you're my age?

'You bought a pineapple,' she said accusingly; the damn thing was sticking out of my shopping cart like a tongue from a child's mouth. 'What are you going to make with that then?'

I had no idea of course, but made up some rubbish about Paul, my grandson, loving pineapple upside-down cake—not that I had either an idea or the inclination to make it.

'Oh,' she said, raising one of her wonkily drawn on eyebrows.

Luckily the rain gave me an excuse to get in, Iris still eyeing the pineapple suspiciously as it made its way down my garden path.

That evening I couldn't settle properly, the usual run of soaps and news holding no interest. He was there, you see. No matter how hard I tried to push him from my mind he was back, staking a claim in my brain and in my heart, and I knew he would not give me a moment's peace. I thought about catching the number 49, seeing if he would be on it, but I knew he wouldn't be. Knowing him and his sense of humour, he took the 49 to confuse me. The more I thought about where he would be, why he was here, the more panicky I became at the thought of not seeing him again.

Stubbs, my dog, rested his greying head on my lap, his brown eyes searching mine. 'I'm finally going mad,' I told Stubbs. He licked my palm.

The next morning I felt better. My anxiety had vanished with the breaking of a new day.

Besides, I had too much to occupy me. My grandson Paul and his new girlfriend Tanya was due round with my great grandchildren, and I had a pineapple to deal with. I sliced it finely and added it to a cake mixture, the juice added to the icing. I was glad to be rid of it.

They arrived promptly at 11. They always arrive promptly, on time. Prompt should be their surname, like in Happy Families.

'Can't stay long,' said Tanya, ushering Jamie and Anna into my living room. 'The kids have a play date.'

'What's that then? A play date?' I asked. I knew the answer; I just wanted to annoy her.

I handed Paul the cake. He sat on the floor with *that* woman and the children, feeding Jamie, who is eight-years-old.

'What's wrong with him?' I asked. 'Surely he knows how to feed himself?'

Paul shot me a look. 'Nothing,' he said, 'it's part of his emotional connection with others. We've been reading about it. Everyone's doing it.'

The Tanya woman looked at me as if I was stupid, as if I had never raised children of my own. I retreated to the couch and sat quietly.

The cake soon eaten, Paul turned his attention to me. 'How are you?' he asked. 'You do look a bit tired,'

I was. I was very tired all the time, and most of all when they came to see me, analysing me like an ant under a magnifying glass.

'I'm fine,' I said, excusing myself to get some more tea.

He was back. In my kitchen now, the sly bugger. I thought he would have left when I got rid of the pineapple, but now here he was, this time in the blue chipped mug on the sideboard. He used to have a mug like that, yet somehow over all these years I had forgotten. He would drink his tea out of it—black with one sugar, always saying it tasted the same as if it had milk in it. He would probably still have that mug: the inside stained brown from the tea, resting on a draining board somewhere else.

I took a deep breath and held onto the counter top, looking at my hands. They used to be pretty hands you know, slender fingers and long nails. My mother used to tell me I had piano playing hands, making me learn just to impress the neighbours. Now they're old and bent hands. The nails are thick and almost yellow; the veins popping to the surface of the paper-thin skin, reminding me that it won't be long now.

They left soon after their second cup and all afternoon I sat with Stubbs on the couch, thinking of a plan to find him. With age everything takes longer.

I was at the library far too early. The bitter wind from the north was still blowing, making my teeth chatter.

'You alright love?' a burly man with a yellow vest asked me as he made his way past into a roadworks ditch. 'Far too cold for you to be waiting here, there's a caff just three doors down you could wait in.' I thanked him and walked towards the café. Hadn't I known it was here all along?

By the time the library opened its doors, I had drunk three cups of bitter tea, and eaten half a stale croissant served to me by a surly looking girl with studs all over her body.

'Why do you do that?' I asked her, pointing at the stud in her cheek.

'Because I can,' she answered.

Walking into the library, I found the information desk.

'I want to use the internet,' I told the man behind the desk. He smiled at me as if I were mad. I didn't take offence though; at my age you get used to people thinking you're mad.

He led me to a computer which was perched on a high table. The only way to use it was to clamber onto a tall metal stool. I did, in a most undignified way with my skirts bunching up around my thighs, and, as I straddled the stool, my arthritic knees and feet screamed with pain.

I don't know what he did. Screen after screen of people's faces, pictures, news, flashed before me.

'I'm sorry, I can't find him,' he said, 'you'd be lucky to find someone that age online anyway.'

As far as I was aware everyone was using the internet. Even Iris was 'socialising' online—whatever that meant.

'I'll come back,' I said to him as I lowered myself off the stool. He smiled at me, kindly this time, and for some reason it made me madder than when he thought I was a dotty old woman.

I wondered if I should have searched for the name, Harry. Instead I had tried his given name of Harold, but he had always hated that, insisted on being called anything else. I sighed; I'd try again the next time, I'd try and find him again, my Harry.

On my way home I stopped by the supermarket. I bought a box of chocolates to cheer myself up, and that's when I saw him again. I was stood at the till, box of chocolates in hand, when he just sauntered past the window, this time wearing a brown coat with a fur collar, a Russian bearskin hat on his head. I dropped the chocolates, all of them skittering across the floor and under the tills.

'I'm so sorry,' I said, not waiting this time but pushing past everyone to get outside, noticing Iris at the other till, her wonky eyebrow raised at me again.

It

is

something

to

have

been

I woke on the day of the funeral lying on my bed, in clothes that were not mine. The black suit was too big—it had been Philip's after all. It was probably wrong to wear a dead man's suit to his own funeral, but I thought that Philip would have appreciated it somehow; besides, I didn't have a black suit, and there was no-one to take me shopping to get one.

I had dressed the night before with some strange romantic notion that just by wearing his suit I would be close to him for a while longer, a little while longer before we had to close the lid and bury him next to Eva.

I got out of bed slowly and stood for a few seconds until my legs felt weak. I grabbed my walking stick, my hand holding onto the handle—the curve of a lion's head—and painfully made my way downstairs. It was time to say goodbye.

The church was packed with faces that seemed familiar to me; hazy, misshapen, sagging, older, but all the same eyes looking at me. The once youthful Millie sat next to her still red-faced husband Gerald, Jilly and Martin had made it from Australia, their son John had turned up, and was not the surly teenager that I remembered. Francis of course was there to pay his respects to his step-father (noticeably lacking his wife); and a few faces I knew, but did not know how to talk to, sat squashed in a pew at the back. My daughter Alison and her daughter Emma and her son Paul had come, which was kind, but the fact was that we really didn't know each other. Alison had tracked me down eventually after Mary had told her everything and we had sat across from each other in a restaurant, politely smiling at each other and making small talk. She brought her daughter Emma with her for moral support I suppose. But her husband had just left her and she did not seem the least bit interested in her new grandfather; instead took advantage of me paying the bill and drank copious amounts of gin.

This handful of meetings over the past five or so years and we were no closer than if we had just met on the bus. A part of me wondered if they were as bad as my son Thomas and were now waiting for my time to come to see if my will showed that they meant anything to me at all.

One face I did not see on the back pew was the one I knew that I would never see again; the face that had haunted me from my early twenties, following me into the war, into the grey churning water, keeping me focused on her rather than the reality. The hours spent on that Scottish island, wishing to see Mary's face again, imagining her with me, wishing that things were different. And now, in this cold church, I was glad I had never seen her again: it would have changed me too much.

I sat on the front pew next to Francis. His hair now grey, I missed the boy he used to be and wished that I had spent more time with him, enjoying his company, his chubby fingers pointing at the flowers, his keen eyes reading all the books in sight.

Philip had wanted an open casket, and I wasn't sure why. Each of us had to walk up to the coffin and take one last look at our friend before he was gone forever. I walked slowly behind Francis, and when I reached Philip I wanted to laugh. Someone somewhere had surely got this wrong? This was not Philip—this waxwork body with garishly painted lips and blush on his cheeks? I looked around the church, but no-one else seemed to think anything was amiss. So this, I thought, is what I would look like when I was dead too. This was death: a painted face. A pretence, a falsification of the person's being.

My legs were struggling to hold me up, so I leaned on the casket, pretending that I was looking closely at my friend. As I did, I noticed a manuscript placed next to him. I looked closer and saw that it was mine, something I had given him a few years ago—my legacy, the only work I had ever been proud of. Philip had said at the time that he didn't think it would sell, then a few months later told me he had lost it. As much as I had been upset at its disappearance, I had trusted his judgement that perhaps my 'life's work' was no more than the ramblings of an old man, an old and second-rate writer.

But now here it was, placed with him to turn to mulch in the ground, to rot along with him. I slowly turned to look at the others who were murmuring amongst themselves. Quickly, I reached in and took the bundle of papers, stuck them under my jacket and slowly walked back to my seat.

'I saw you,' Francis whispered to me. I didn't look at him. He took hold of my arm and squeezed reassuringly.

'Why do they call it a wake?' Millie asked, her voice still irritatingly girlish although she was well into her 90s. 'I mean, it's not like he's going to wake up is he? I mean, he's dead.'

I sat across from her and nodded along. The sheaf of papers was still hidden under my jacket.

'Technically,' Gerald boomed, his frail body still holding that giant voice, 'a wake is before a funeral. Supposed to stay awake with the body overnight and pray and whatnot.'

'So, what do you call this then?' Millie asked. 'A party?'

'Buggered if I know,' Gerald said refilling his glass of whisky. 'Doesn't really matter does it? He's dead and we're next. Really it's a practice run for us. Help us get some ideas for what we want at ours!'

'Oh Gerald, you're so morbid!' Millie play-hit her husband.

I had offered my house as the venue for the wake, or party, as Millie said. It was bigger than Philip's house and I had said I would pay for the catering too, which had pleased everyone.

I watched Francis standing in the corner talking to Alison and Emma. I did not want to speak to them; they would be kind and offer to have me over for dinner, I knew. But I wanted to be alone now. It was all just too late.

I grabbed snippets from his conversation: '...thought it was his best work, but of course it would have embarrassed us all. He knew it could never get published.'

'They were fictional though weren't they?' my daughter asked.

'Not overly,' Francis answered.

I stood up slowly, resting most of my weight on my stick, and moved toward them to hear more; but as I got closer, they changed the subject.

'What about all his books?' she asked.

'I'll sort them,' Francis raked a hand through his hair. 'It'll take a while. He has masses. Always did.'

I coughed but none of them looked at me. Francis had probably told them that I had taken my manuscript back. I thought they were being childish. If Philip had thought it was my best work, as Francis had said, then I had been right to take it with me instead of letting it be buried away. Philip had, after all, stolen my words.

I shuffled away from them, not wanting to start an argument at a time like this, and found myself in my study gazing at my battered typewriter on my desk, a few hurried notes, barely legible on a pad next to it. I sat down in my chair and finally took the manuscript out of my jacket. I smoothed the papers flat and looked at my title:

> The Truth And The Lies: *A semi-autobiographical novel by Harry Winter.*

The title was all wrong, as was the pronouncement that it was semi-autobiographical; Francis and Philip were right it would have ruined them all. I took a fresh piece of paper and stuck it into the typewriter. I would change it; this could still work; this could still be my legacy.

The Last Step

The winter was long in passing. Harold sat in his favourite armchair watching the hail pelt his beloved garden; the television was on mute, showing an afternoon chat show where families shouted at one another. Harold didn't care much for shouting.

He looked at the stacks of books dotted about the room, at the papers, notes, battered manuscripts and knew he should write or read something. He inspected his hands: his fingers were knobbly and crooked from arthritis. He picked up a pen and pad from his table and tried to write his name but his fingers could not hold the pen strongly enough so his name became a squiggle and a line of ink.

His old speckled hands rubbed at his knees. He needed to move. He stood slowly, leaning on the armchair for support, then let go and wobbled slightly so he grabbed onto the mantelpiece. Little by little, using furniture to aid him, he shuffled across the room. He reached the patio doors, and watched as his warm hands, pressed on the cold glass, made steamy handprints.

Five stone steps which he had laid fifty years ago with his nephew led down into his oasis of a trimmed lawn, sculpted hedges and pruned rose bushes. A pond filled with orange goldfish and red-and-white koi sat at the bottom of the garden; a hammock, fixed between the apple and pear tree, hung forlornly as the hail showered down.

'What are you doing?' a voice behind him asked.

The sudden noise made him wobble, and his handprints smeared on the glass. Janice ran across the room and grabbed him roughly under his armpits. 'What on earth were you thinking?' she said.

He tried to walk, but Janice was strong, and as she forcefully helped him his slippered feet dragged across the thick blue carpet.

'There that's better isn't it? How about I make you a cup of tea?'

He didn't respond.

'Tea?' she asked again, this time not waiting for a reply before walking away into the kitchen.

Janice had been with him for eight months. She had arrived with his son Craig on a warm summer's evening, just after his fall. 'This is Janice,' he was told of the stocky fifty-something woman stood on his doorstep, 'and she's here to mind you. To watch you don't fall again,' his son had said, looking guilty.

Falling again wasn't an option with Janice around. She didn't allow him to move often, so his legs, weak with age anyway, were made weaker with the lack of exercise. He missed moving, he thought. He missed coffee. He missed his garden.

Janice reappeared with his tea, placed it on his side table and tucked a blanket around his legs.

'I'm not cold,' he said.

She ignored him and tucked the blanket tighter. 'What would you do without me eh?' She stood in front of him with her hands on her hips, and her head cocked to one side. She reminded him of the fat robin that came every winter. The robin hadn't been this year. He missed the robin.

'Yes Janice, what would I do?' He waited until she bundled herself back into the kitchen, pulled the blanket off his knees and picked up Dr Flaberman's book of wildflowers. The book was old now, its red leather cover bruised with age, and the well-thumbed pages yellow and mottled brown. His father had given it to him on his tenth birthday, and ever since then he had re-read it, made notes in the margin and circled flowers that he had found and planted in his own garden.

'You reading that old thing again?'

He looked up to see Janice walking towards him with his dinner on a tray. It wasn't yet three o'clock.

'I'm not hungry Janice,' he said. He didn't lift his face from the book.

She placed the tray on his lap and started to cut up the meat.

He put the book on the side table and sat still in his chair. The sound of the knife scraping the white china plate made him grind his back teeth.

'Now come on,' she had a forkful ready for him, 'open up.'

As the fork made its way to his mouth, he lifted the tray off his lap and tipped it onto the floor. At first, she didn't notice and tried to feed him even though his mouth was closed. But the gravy had splattered her fat stockinged legs, and she screamed when she felt the heat. She ran into the kitchen.

'Are you okay?' he asked. He picked up the book.

She returned with a tea towel and cleared away the mess of food on the floor. Then she stood up and walked back into the kitchen. Harold could hear the banging of cupboard doors as she fixed him another meal.

He read until he fell asleep, then woke to Janice gently tapping his shoulder. 'You okay there?' she said. She placed another tray in front of him, this time on a small table. 'Now then, don't spill this one.'

He looked at the meal—his favourite, a meat and potato pie. His stomach grumbled.

'I hope you like it.' She looked at him and smiled tightly.

He ate all of his meal, and by the time he had finished, he felt almost guilty for what he had done earlier.

'Was it okay?' she asked him, as she picked up the plate.

'Absolutely wonderful.' He smiled at her.

'I'll be off shortly.'

'Okay,' he said, and picked up his book.

'I was thinking though, that I ought to call Craig?' She cocked her head to the side again.

'Why?' He put his book down.

'Oh you know, just to let him know how weak your legs are getting. I'm a bit worried since you can't balance a tray on them.'

'Now look here Janice, my legs are just fine!' He spat the words at her.

'Oh Harold,' she said, sighing. She walked away from him, shaking her head.

Within minutes, she was back: purple coat on, bag in hand. He didn't look at her and instead fixed his stare on the mantelpiece.

'I'll be off, Harold. I'll see you later for bedtime. I've called Craig. He says he will call me later at home to discuss how we are going to move forward.' She came over and tucked the blanket over his legs again.

'I'm not cold,' he said.

She ignored him. 'He did mention me moving in here with you. Wouldn't that be nice?'

Harold looked at her, and she smiled. She turned from him and walked out the front door, humming a tune to herself.

He waited until he heard the crunch of tyres on the gravelled driveway, then eased himself out of his chair. Leaning on pieces of furniture he made it back to the patio doors. The hail had stopped, leaving his garden wet and battered. He stood for a while, watching the weak winter sun set, the dark slowly creeping over his garden until he could not see anything. He hung his head. The old grandfather clock loudly chimed six. Normally, he would make himself a small whiskey, turn on the radio and spend the next few hours listening to the classics or a play. Instead, he edged his way into the kitchen. He knew it was here somewhere.

He opened all the cupboards but couldn't find what he was looking for. He pulled out a kitchen chair from the table and sat for a moment thinking. If he was Janice, where would he put it, he wondered? The clock chimed quarter past, and he realised where it was. He shuffled into the pantry, and there, hidden at the back, was his walking stick.

She took it away a few weeks ago when she found him stepping slowly down the garden steps. He had watched helplessly as she walked into the kitchen with it, then he had suffered her strong hands guiding him back to his chair ever since.

He took the stick in his hand. The handle, carved into a lion's head—its eyes set with amethysts. He noticed the left eye was now a black hole; the right still had the amethyst, but it was loose, turning in the socket as he touched it with his finger.

Using the stick, he walked steadily through the kitchen to the patio doors. He switched on the outdoor lights, and with his right hand unlocked the doors and slid them open. The cold night air rushed in at him and took his breath away. He breathed in deeply and exhaled, watching his breath hang in the air. He smiled and took a step outside.

A mist covered the garden and even with the bright outdoor lights, he couldn't see where his fish bobbed and swam in their pond. He knew they were there somewhere. He walked forward towards the steps, placed his stick on the first step and eased himself down.

The call of a wood pigeon filled his ears, and he stood with his eyes closed listening for the call of its mate.

The second step down was easier for him. A tub of wildflowers sat at one end; the colour of the Winter Heliotrope and early crocuses reminded him of the purple of Janice's coat. He took another step down.

He heard the chime of the clock alerting him to the fact it was now seven. He wondered where the time had gone.

He looked at the sky. It was a clear night, and the blue-black was pinpricked with stars. The moon was in its last quarter. He would have liked to have seen a full moon.

He took another step down onto the last step. It was higher than the others and slightly uneven. He had tripped and fallen off it many times onto the paving stones below that edged around the lawn. He let go of his stick. With one leg, he stepped out to test his balance and wobbled violently. His heart beat hard in his chest, and he placed his foot back on the step, slowly bent down and retrieved his stick.

He turned around and made his way back up the steps. He reached the living room: it was quarter past, he didn't have much time.

He switched off the outdoor light and stepped back onto the patio; it was completely black. He had expected that the glow from the neighbours' houses would shed some light, but looking left and right, he saw that they were dark.

He used his stick, as a blind person would use their cane, to gauge where he was and the location of the steps.

His arm was tiring now from holding himself up, and his knees groaned with pain. With each step down, he wobbled, and twice he had to sit down to calm himself.

He reached the last step and waited until he heard the clock chime eight.

Harold dropped the walking stick on the ground in front of him and breathed in deeply. He could feel how weak his legs were and how they shook trying to hold his body up. Instinctively he held his arms in front of him; feeling the night air for something to hold onto.

He made himself stand as still as he could, putting his arms resolutely by his side, and looked at the sky and said a silent prayer.

With a smile on his face, Harold took the last step out into the night.

The Great Minimum

It is something to have wept as we have wept,
It is something to have done as we have done,
It is something to have watched when all men slept,
And seen the stars which never see the sun.

It is something to have smelt the mystic rose,
Although it break and leave the thorny rods,
It is something to have hungered once as those
Must hunger who have ate the bread of gods.

To have seen you and your unforgotten face,
Brave as a blast of trumpets for the fray,
Pure as white lilies in a watery space,
It were something, though you went from me today.

To have known the things that from the weak are furled,
erilous ancient passions, strange and high;
It is something to be wiser than the world,
It is something to be older than the sky.

In a time of sceptic moths and cynic rusts,
And fattened lives that of their sweetness tire
In a world of flying loves and fading lusts,
It is something to be sure of a desire.

Lo, blessed are our ears for they have heard;
Yea, blessed are our eyes for they have seen:
Let the thunder break on man and beast and bird
And the lightning. It is something to have been.

G. K. Chesterton